A MESSAGE FROM CHICKEN HOUSE

Yⁿou'll love this story of wild and unpredictable Tiggy! Her story starts when her little brother is kidnapped by the Pirate King alongside all the boys of her island. Undeterred – even by the Pirate King's fearsome giant squid! – Tiggy and her pals set off in pursuit.

Thanks to her courage and fierce friendships she discovers the secrets of the folk beneath the sea and claims her destiny – but can she save her brother? Anna and Oli are a unique pair of rambunctious talents – I had to hold their imagination by its collar, but you can run away with it now!

BARRY CUNNINGHAM
Publisher
Chicken House

Antigua de Fortune of the High Seas

ANNA RAINBOW & OLI HYATT

Chicken House

2 PALMER STREET, FROME, SOMERSET BA11 1DS

Written by Oli Hyatt and Anna Day
Copyright Oli Hyatt © 2021
Illustration © Paola Escobar 2021

First published in Great Britain in 2021
Chicken House
2 Palmer Street
Frome, Somerset BA11 1DS
United Kingdom
www.chickenhousebooks.com

Cover and interior design by Steve Wells
Typeset by Dorchester Typesetting Group Ltd
Printed and bound in Great Britain by CPI Group (UK) Ltd, Croydon, CR0 4YY

For my family. Simon, Ellie, Charlie and Fern.
A.R.

For anyone who has a story to tell, but no voice,
and to the people who help them speak.
O.H.

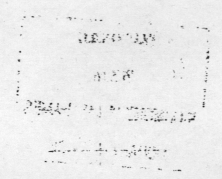

CHAPTER 1

Tiggy strode down the harbour, lifting her skirts so the sea breeze cooled her ankles. Since turning five, her brother, Diego, had refused to hold her hand in public, yet he happily walked beside her, his linen pouch of stacking stones cradled in his arms like a chest of treasure. She could sense the excitement in his step. Today marked the beginning of the Bloodmoon celebrations; three days dedicated to feasting, dancing and dressing up as sea creatures. Somehow, her good friend, Felipe – her best friend's older brother – matched their pace, though he had to trail his fishing rod behind him. The rhythmic clunk of his wooden leg against the planks always soothed Tiggy, like the tick of a watch or the click of beetles at night.

The trio stopped only when they reached the edge of the pier so the sea surrounded them on all sides. Panting slightly, Tiggy pulled off her boots and dangled her feet in the water. She sighed and imagined her legs were hollow reeds, that she could somehow suck the ocean into her body, starting from her toes.

Diego knelt and began to play, the soft clack of his stones mixing with the lap of waves.

'Good idea,' Felipe said as he plonked himself beside Tiggy and pretended to pinch his nose. 'I didn't know quite how to tell you, but those feet of yours...'

Tiggy shoved an elbow into his ribs, a laugh escaping into the briny air. 'Seriously, if you had to wear all these stupid petticoats, you'd sweat like a cuttlefish too.' She pulled a small wooden case from her pocket and clicked it open.

Diego peered over her shoulder. 'Gross.'

The maggots squirmed around each other like podgy little snakes, gleaming in the sun. Tiggy picked out two of the juiciest and handed them to her friend.

'Cuttlefish don't sweat.' Felipe skewered the creamy blobs of flesh on to the silver hook.

'I have it on good authority that they do indeed,' Tiggy replied.

'Yeah? Off who?'

'Er . . . your very own madre told me, and let's face it, she'd know.'

Embarrassment flickered beneath Felipe's features and he cast his line into the water a little too vigorously, as though trying to rid himself of some uncomfortable feeling. Tiggy could have kicked herself. She knew that Felipe loved his mum, but any reference to her selkie background always made his cheeks redden. Funnily enough, Tiggy wished *her* mum was selkie-born because, being female, that might make Tiggy of selkie blood too, and imagine being able to turn into a seal at will. She briefly wondered if she'd ever bother turning back again. Maybe she would live out at sea for ever. She gazed longingly across the blue of the ocean, watching the sun as it fell slowly through the sky. Did it long to sink into those cool, cool waters too? She could almost hear the blissful fizz of the flames extinguishing.

'Madre isn't the oracle of the ocean, you know,' Felipe eventually mumbled. 'And cuttlefish don't sweat. They just don't. I mean, they haven't even got skin.'

'They have too,' Diego piped up. 'Slimy fish skin that smells of turtle poo.'

Before Tiggy could recite Madre's words (*Now, Diego, nobody wants to think about poo*), she heard footsteps approaching from behind. She turned to see Lucia, an ex-pirate and captain of a run-down trading ship, renowned for keeping her motley crew in line with harsh words and bribes of rum. Lucia towered over them, the port spreading behind her like a colourful cape: boats tethered and bobbing in the breeze, galleons threatening to capsize anything which stood in their way, men unloading cargo and the flash of coins changing hands. Tiggy could smell the faint bite of liquor, hear the roar of drunkards from the taverns.

'You shouldn't be dipping your toes in the ocean, Antigua,' Lucia said, using Tiggy's full name. Her accent was thick with kindness and faraway adventures in other lands. 'You know those waves are filled with mischief.'

'Today of all days, I refuse to fear the ocean,' Tiggy replied.

Lucia adjusted her headcloth, causing her braid to slide across her shoulder like a black rope. 'Don't let the Bloodmoon celebrations lull you into a false sense of security, Antigua – sharks can bite any day of the year. Isn't that right, Felipe?'

Felipe grunted. He had never told Tiggy how he lost his leg, but rumour suggested it had something to do with a hungry shark and a merman.

'Anyway,' Lucia said, 'it's the annual Golem Ball tonight, isn't it?'

Now it was Tiggy's turn to grunt. She couldn't bear the thought of the Golem Ball. This year, it meant she would be paraded before the Governor like a prize goat, whilst his vile son, Salvador, looked her up and down and mentally measured her for bridal gear. For the love of Kraken, she was only fourteen. She edged a little closer to the sea, letting the waters inhale her ankles and calves, thinking that perhaps a hungry shark wouldn't be such an unfortunate fate after all.

Diego lifted his head from his stones and forced his voice into an indignant squeak, which Tiggy assumed was supposed to sound like her: *I don't want to talk about it. Balls are rubbish and Salvador is a sweaty pig.*

'Diego, quiet.' Tiggy poked him in the ribs.

'Oh, come on,' Lucia said, ignoring Diego's squeals of delight. 'It won't be so bad. You'll be in the Governor's house after all. You can stuff your face with fancy food, eat from silver dinner plates, heck, find his gold and stash it up your skirts. And if your conscience raises its ugly head, give the loot to my crew. Kraken knows we could do with it.' Her cackle was infectious, causing Tiggy and Felipe to giggle too.

Lucia gestured to the water below, fear zipping across her dark features and eliminating her smile in an instant. 'Just don't say I didn't warn you, Antigua de Fortune, for gone are the days when man was welcomed by the sea.' And with that, she turned and sidled back up the pier, her long shadow sashaying after her.

Tiggy felt a flutter of jealousy in her chest. She wished she could wear breeches, braid her hair and sail the high seas. But no. She had to go to a stupid ball and dance with stupid Salvador. She slumped, watching the gulls pick at the fish as steadily as the frustration picked at her heart.

Eventually, Felipe tugged the fruitless line from the water, tutting at the drowned maggots like it was their fault they weren't juicy enough. 'Come on, then. Your madre will string me up if you're late tonight.'

'But we didn't catch anything,' Tiggy said.

Diego didn't miss a beat. 'You never do.'

She pulled on her shoes, helped Diego pick up his stones and then drifted back up the pier, enjoying one last lungful of salty air. The trio passed the smaller boats where crews lounged on upturned barrels, the stink of sweat and *vino seco* hanging around them like a swarm of flies. They reached the port where they were dipped in shadow by the larger galleons and swept up by the bustle of brawny, sea-worn men lugging sacks of sugar cane and cochineal. By the time they'd wound their way through the various stalls and taverns, listening to the cries of the sellers and the laughter of the sailors, the sky was beginning to lose some of its heat.

Felipe paused beneath a sign boasting a picture of a seal reclining on a rock; the words above its fawn head read: *The Signum Tavern*. Felipe gestured to the door. 'Do you want to come inside for a second? Marina will want to see you.'

Diego tugged at her skirt, a silent indication that he wanted to go home to his supper. Tiggy sighed.

Marina, Felipe's younger sister, was Tiggy's best friend, and usually they were inseparable. But since Marina had failed to receive an invite to the Golem Ball, she'd distanced herself a little – forgetting to call at Tiggy's house, or being 'too tired' to go fishing.

Tiggy knew that Marina longed to wear those ridiculous frocks and to dance with Salvador, yet as the daughter of a barmaid and suspected selkie, she was destined to remain anchored firmly to the port. If only Tiggy and Marina could swap lives, they would both be happier. Something painful and hot pierced her heart. *And so would Madre*, she thought. *She would finally get the daughter she wanted.* Tears welled in her eyes and her throat ached with the effort of holding them in.

'Tiggy?' Felipe said, jolting her from her thoughts.

'Er, no. I better leave it a day or so.'

Felipe brushed her hand, so gently it felt like a moth's wing. 'She'll get over it,' he said. 'After the ball, she'll be back to her annoying self. And she won't miss tomorrow night's celebration for anything, so you'll see her there.'

Tiggy studied his face. He had definitely changed since returning from sea last year. He still had the same olive skin, the same denim dungarees and ready smile, yet his face looked stronger, his eyes more knowing. Perhaps he just looked older. 'Thanks, Felipe,' she said, pulling an angry hand across her telltale eyes.

He slipped inside the tavern and she was left with a very impatient brother. 'Come on, Tig. The kraken is rumbling inside my tummy.'

'That means nothing, you're always hungry – the kraken lives permanently inside your tummy.'

'Is that why I can't go to the Golem Ball?' His bottom lip began to protrude. 'Because my tummy is too noisy?'

She rested her hand on his wind-tousled hair. 'Of course not, it's because you're too young.'

'But I want to go too. I want to wear a mask and steal the Governor's gold.'

'Lucia was joking. Nobody's stealing anything.'

'Not even the fancy food?' A note of sadness ran through his voice, causing Tiggy's heart to swell.

'Look.' She held his gaze. 'It's like Felipe said, tomorrow night we'll dress up as ghouls of the sea and go knocking on the neighbours' doors, asking for honeyed fruits and pots of jam. You'll forget all about the Golem Ball then.'

Diego's face lit up and he started dancing on his tiptoes, as if the cobbles had been replaced with hot coals. 'And the beach carnival, tell me about the beach carnival.'

'Well, that's the day after tomorrow, on Bloodmoon Day. There's going to be an actual Bloodmoon eclipse where the full moon turns from pearl to crimson, as though she were dunked in the blood of the Pirate King himself. It will be the first in fifty years, Diego, imagine that? And there's going to be a carnival on the beach, with costumes and fireworks and cannons . . .' She waved her hands in the air, pumping her fists open and closed, painting explosions in his mind's eye. 'And the biggest band you've ever heard. Madre promised I could take you, so long as we stay out of the waves. It's going to be so much fun, we'll tell our children about it – *and* our children's children.'

'Will there be whipped sugar?' His eyes twinkled with the thought of it.

'More than we can eat.'

He gnashed his teeth and made chomping noises, all thoughts of the Golem Ball replaced with the promise of the sweet taste of sticky beet.

Tiggy laughed. 'Come on, we best get home.'

They turned towards the town. The maze of houses seemed to have grown from the cliff face itself, lining the twisting streets and rocky steps with their peach and yellow faces, dwindling in numbers into the green of the hills, where the air lay cool and moist and only the rich folk lived. Beyond, the mountains clawed up the sky, lava simmering in their vast, lazy bellies like a dark secret just waiting to erupt. It seemed fitting that the island was called Haven; it truly was a slice of paradise. So why did it never quite feel like home?

'Come on, slowboat.' She clipped her brother gently round his crown. 'Madre will be pacing the floors by now.'

'Slowboat?' Diego exclaimed. 'I'm faster than you any day.'

'You reckon?' Tiggy hitched up her skirt, demonstrating her readiness to race.

Diego glanced at his pouch of stones. 'No fair, I'm carrying rocks and I've only got little legs.'

'Rocks? They look more like pebbles to me.' But she stretched out her hands all the same, allowing him to dump the collection in her arms. She then watched him race towards the hills, his laughter tumbling down the path as he ran. She couldn't help but smile as she began to follow him up the track to Madre, to her ridiculous frock – and to the arms of the vile Salvador.

CHAPTER 2

Tiggy stood in front of the full-length mirror, her lips curled in disgust. 'You want me to wear *this*?'

Her mother didn't reply; rather she proceeded to buzz around her daughter like an annoying mosquito, flumping up the frills and smoothing out the pleats as though she could somehow carve the perfect frock with her hands.

'Madre, please,' Tiggy pleaded. 'I look like a mango.' She pulled helplessly at the folds of peach silk. 'Worse. I look like a mango that met a canary and had an orange bird baby.'

Finally, Madre straightened up. She was a tall woman and always used her height to her advantage, looking down her nose at everyone. She stared at Tiggy with two heavily lashed eyes and – tucking a mahogany curl back into her bun – sighed loudly, as if the air in her lungs tasted sour. 'You do not look like an orange bird baby.' A smile touched her lips, yet slid away so fast Tiggy wondered if she'd imagined it. Madre picked a black ringlet from Tiggy's shoulder. 'Everything is perfect – except for your hair, where a laurel pigeon has surely nested. Why couldn't you have stayed inside, today of all days?'

The heat of the sun, the sea spray and the constant supply of sweat had transformed Tiggy's already unruly hair into a black mass of curls. 'I kind of like it,' Tiggy said.

'It's not just your hair. It's . . .' Madre paused, selecting her words with care. 'Man isn't welcomed by the sea, not since the reign of the Pirate King. The sharks are hungrier, the fish people angrier. I only trust the selkies because of, well, you know . . .' She tailed off, even though Tiggy already knew why – Madre had long been friends with Felipe's madre, Gabriella.

Tiggy sighed. 'They're called merfolk, Madre, not fish people.'

'Well, whatever you call them, the fact remains that the harbour is no place for a young lady like yourself.'

Tiggy suppressed a wave of annoyance. She had heard this a hundred times before. When would Madre realize that being near the sea made her feel complete? And surely not all merfolk were hostile – the Pirate King had died a long time ago, after all. She watched Madre fetch a mother-of-pearl comb from her dressing table. The opalescent teeth glinted in the fading evening sun. *I'm going to hurt you*, they said. 'I'll do it,' she sang out, reaching for the weapon. But Madre whipped it away, causing her daughter's hand to sail empty through the air.

An expression of determination locked into Madre's usually soft features and she bit down on her lip. 'Consider this your penance, Antigua de Fortune.' She sank the comb into her daughter's head.

The teeth scraped against Tiggy's scalp and delivered a surge of pain as they snagged against a wall of knots. 'Ow,' she wailed, clutching her hand to her head. 'Do you want me to be bald?'

Madre caught Tiggy's eye in the mirror and offered the most fleeting of winks. 'Maybe.'

As her mother continued to haul the comb through the mist of curls, Tiggy felt sure her skin would peel clean away, revealing the shiny bone of her skull. At least then Salvador would leave her be.

Summoned by the yelps of pain, her padre opened the bedroom door, his face shaped by concern. 'What's going on?'

Diego surfaced behind his father; he was already wearing his favourite striped nightgown and his favourite wicked grin.

'Padre, you have to save me,' Tiggy managed to splutter. 'Madre is trying to kill me.'

Padre laughed, his mouth twisting sideways like a camel chewing on grass. He wagged a playful finger at Madre. 'Now, now, you know the house rules, Señora de Fortune. No child murder before sundown.'

'No child murder *ever*,' Diego said.

Even though her scalp burnt, Tiggy found it impossible to quell the laughter which bubbled from her stomach. 'Padre, I am not joking, she's turned wild.'

Padre slipped into the room. He was a tall, slim man with the straightest back Tiggy had ever seen; it was as though his spine had set in Naval officer-pose: standing to attention on the bow of his galleon, telescope pressed to one eye. He had the strong face of the Naval officer he was, thatched with greying black hair, though he insisted that after fourteen years of Naval duty, the grey was simply sea salt permanently crusted on to his head.

He took an admiring glance at his daughter. 'Well, being murdered suits you, darling. You look stunning.'

'I look like—' Tiggy began, but Madre finished her sentence with a gleeful tone. 'A mango met a canary and had an orange bird baby.'

Diego ran up to her, a grin spreading across his face. 'You look hilarious.'

'Diego,' Madre scalded.

But he ignored his mother's tone and ducked low, fluffing up the fabric of Tiggy's skirt and somehow managing to crawl around her ankles so he too was inside the dress. 'I'm stuck inside a giant peach,' he called, pushing his hands against the material and causing the frock to look as though it were alive. 'Help, I'm stuck.'

Tiggy watched in the mirror as her skirt flapped and billowed, occasionally revealing the shape of a wriggling boy. Laughter spilt from her mouth, and for a blissful moment she forgot about the stupid ball. If only she could take Diego with her, at least then the night would be slightly less intolerable.

'Diego,' Madre shrieked, 'you're going to rip it.' She hauled her son clear of the fabric. 'Now get to bed or I swear, the Pirate King will steal you away and turn you into a Sea Golem.'

He laughed. 'I wish I was a Sea Golem, then I wouldn't have to tidy my room.'

'You shouldn't joke about the stolen boys of Haven,' Madre said, pointing a finger at him.

But Diego was already dancing out of the door, singing about Sea Golems and leaving the room behind him noticeably quieter.

After a long pause, Padre finally spoke. 'The frock is very … peach.' He laid the back of his hand against Tiggy's cheek. 'But it brings out the lovely tone of your skin.'

Tiggy tentatively allowed her eyes to travel up her reflection. He had a point. Her skin looked darker against the peach, so that at a glance she could have been a native to the Fortune Isles rather than the daughter of a Naval officer. She liked the idea of having the island running through her veins. The ocean in her blood. Even if she did look like a hilarious orange bird baby.

'Ah!' Padre exclaimed, reaching inside his fitted jacket. 'I almost forgot . . . the icing on the cake.' He pulled out three eye masks. 'Which one do you want?'

Each was moulded from papier mâché and hardened with metallic paints and jewels. They offered mystery, intrigue, a chance to be somebody else entirely; excitement began to smoulder in Tiggy's chest, briefly overshadowing any thoughts of Salvador and her stupid dress. She studied them in turn. The first was a golden crab, its pincers rearing from either side of the eye holes so that whoever wore it would look like they'd grown horns. The second was a mermaid, pitted with dozens of tiny rainbow scales, with threads of black silk which sprouted from its sides to give the illusion of tumbling raven locks.

The final mask – a jumble of barnacles and cracked clay – was edged with dried seaweed. *A Sea Golem*, she thought, curbing a shudder. 'I thought we weren't supposed to joke about the stolen boys of Haven.'

Madre shot her a serious look. 'That's right, Antigua.'

'We're *honouring* the stolen boys,' Padre said gently. 'Reminding ourselves of the terrible fate they suffered so many years ago, and how lucky we are that the curse has been lifted.'

Despite Padre's reassurance, the decision was easy: Tiggy had no desire to sport barnacles and seaweed on her face, and she'd never shared her fellow Islanders' distaste for merfolk; indeed, ever since she was small, she'd dreamt of breathing under water and darting through the waves with an elegant fish tail of her own. So with deft, hungry fingers, she lifted the mermaid mask from Padre's hands and tied it to her face, enjoying the gentle press of mâché and the prospect of being someone else entirely.

'Is there time to kiss Diego goodnight?' she asked Padre, who was far more likely than Madre to say yes.

True to form, he nodded. 'Soon as Madre's finished your hair.'

Tiggy winced. She'd forgotten about the comb of doom.

One very sore scalp later, she stuck her head around Diego's bedroom door; the scent of freshly picked flowers and wooden toy boxes flooded her nose. Rather than lying in bed, her little brother sat cross-legged on his bedroom carpet, lining up his little tin soldiers so they formed a small barrier between the bed and the entrance. He glanced up at the sound of creaking hinges, his face tighter than Tiggy expected. Any Golem-related bravado had flaked from his body like the skin of a snake, leaving behind a tiny five-year-old boy. 'I don't want the Pirate King to get me,' he said simply.

She knelt opposite him and helped straighten the wonkiest of the platoon. 'The Pirate King has been dead for hundreds of years, silly guppy.'

'He'll steal me away and turn me into a Sea Golem, that's what Madre said.' They locked eyes as Diego silently dared his sister to contradict the Law of Mother.

Tiggy smiled. 'That's just something grown-ups say to get children to do what they want. Everyone knows that Sea Golems don't exist any more – the curse of Haven died alongside the Pirate King centuries ago.' She pulled him up and ushered him towards the bed. 'Come on now, off to sleep.'

He clambered beneath his quilt, grabbed Bobo – his one-eyed teddy bear – and watched as Tiggy turned down the lamp, wrapping the room in shadow and the scent of tallow wax.

'There now,' she muttered, perching on the edge of the mattress so she could stroke his cheek. His skin felt warm and familiar, and the longing to stay at home that night, snuggled beneath a blanket with Diego, rose like a song inside her.

'Tell me the story of the Pirate King and the Bloodmoon,' Diego whispered.

She shook her head. 'I'm not terrifying you just before I leave. The maid will crucify me.'

'But I'll stop being scared if you tell me the ending.' Anticipation glinted in his eyes.

She sighed, yet any reluctance was fleeting – missing some of the ball was actually quite appealing. 'OK. But I'm blaming you if we're late.'

'Deal.'

She lay beside him so he could nuzzle his head into her shoulder, then, lowering her voice so it dripped with secrecy and chimed like an ancient spell, she began the familiar tale. 'Legend has it that many centuries ago, a powerful mage terrorized the high seas.'

'The Pirate King,' Diego said, arching his hand so it resembled a hook.

'That's right. The Pirate King was a mage so powerful, he was able to use the sorcery of the ocean against the land. He enticed other pirates to join his ranks, then he persuaded the merfolk and selkies that man was the enemy, and he enchanted innocent sea creatures to do his evil bidding. The waves became a place of death and danger as the Pirate King and his saltwater army capsized our boats, stole our cargo and watched as our men drowned.'

'Is that why Madre won't let me in the sea?'

'That's right. Even now, the sea creatures remain distrustful of man. The Pirate King left quite the legacy.'

'Which leg did he leave at sea?'

Tiggy laughed. 'No, no, he left a *legacy*. It means that what he did – his story – lives on even after his death.' She paused, studying Diego's expression for any signs of fear, but his worries had clearly been replaced by a fascination with all things dark.

'Go on,' he urged.

She grinned, beginning to enjoy the story herself. 'But magical sea creatures, sharks and whales weren't enough for the Pirate King. He wanted his army to be stronger, better. He had the sea . . . he wanted the land. So he placed a curse upon Haven, a curse which allowed him to transform our boys into mindless sea drones, unable to resist his command.'

Diego ducked beneath the covers. 'Sea Golems,' he squeaked with mock terror.

'The Pirate King and his men stormed our beaches and stole our boys, time and time again, plucking them from their beds as they slept.' She whipped the covers from Diego's head, causing him to shriek and kick his legs.

'You can't have me, Pirate King,' he said to Bobo, pretending his bear was the villain himself and flicking him on his black button nose. 'I will bop you in the face and make you cry.'

Tiggy pulled him and the bear closer. 'Sea Golems are horrifying creatures . . . half-child, half-monster, with dark green skin covered in barnacles, webbed fingers and toes, and gills which open beneath their armpits as if they've been slashed by a swordfish.' She tickled his ribs and peals of giggles erupted from Diego's mouth. 'And the worst part?' She leant in, her voice a bare murmur for maximum drama. 'Do you want to know the worst part?'

'What?' His eyes were like dinner plates.

'They forgot they were human and became unfeeling zombies of the sea. They forgot their families and friends, the feeling of sand beneath their feet and the wind in their hair. And without batting an eyelid, they would attack the boats of their fathers and watch on, unflinching, as their loved ones drowned.'

'Get to the good bit,' Diego said. 'Please, please, please.'

She laughed. 'I thought Sea Golems *were* the good bit.'

'No, no, the Bloodmoon. Tell me about the Bloodmoon.'

Madre's voice drifted up the stairs. 'Antigua, time to go. The carriage is waiting.'

Tiggy dropped a light kiss on her brother's head. 'Another time. I've got to go.'

His little hand gripped hers with surprising strength. 'Please, or I'll keep feeling scared, and then the maid will croon to you.'

'Croon to me?'

'That's what you said,' he replied. 'The maid will croon to you, and I don't want that, she's a terrible singer.'

Tiggy chuckled. 'I said she'd *crucify* me.'

'Just tell me,' he begged.

Again, she checked his face for any signs of fear – he looked anything but scared, and Tiggy had never been any good at saying no to those big, dinner-plate eyes, so she tucked the quilt around his shoulders and quickly said, 'After twenty years of terror, a group of brave folk defeated the Pirate King, driving a knife through his black, black heart. The ocean ran crimson with the blood of the deadly mage. Legend says that even the moon turned red.'

'The Bloodmoon,' he said.

She nodded. 'The curse of Haven lifted and not a single child has been stolen from our land since that day. Every year, we mark this with the Bloodmoon celebrations.' A sigh escaped her lips. 'Which is why I have to go to this stupid ball tonight.'

Right on cue, Madre hollered up the stairs, 'Antigua, time to go.'

Tiggy planted another kiss on her little brother's cheek and stood to leave.

'Wait,' Diego said. 'Is it true?' His voice contained both hope and the judder of fear.

Tiggy paused. It was a story woven into the fabric of their community, passed down from parent to child, enacted in school plays, sung of in taverns and nurseries across the island. Was it true? Some of it perhaps. She kissed Diego on the cheek and whispered, 'Of course, silly guppy.' Because every child should believe in the magic of the ocean and the triumph of good over evil. And every child should enjoy the Bloodmoon celebrations with the tremor of possibility in the pit of their stomachs.

His eyelids heavy, Diego clocked the mask in her hand. 'A mermaid? That's a funny choice.'

'Why?'

'They're kind of pretty. I bet Salvador thinks so too.'

Tiggy touched her hand to his head. 'Thanks, Diego.'

She dashed down the stairs and pushed the mermaid mask into Madre's hands. 'I changed my mind. I want to be the Sea Golem.'

CHAPTER 3

Her mane pinned neatly on top of her head and her Golem mask tied to her face, Tiggy arrived at the front of the Governor's manor, sandwiched between her parents and feeling more like a lamb to the slaughter than ever before. The horses trotted into the distance and the trundle of the carriage faded, revealing the wavering notes of a string quartet. Tiggy looked at the manor and sighed. Was it possible for a house to look smug? She believed it was.

Her parents marched her up the stone steps and

through the grand oak doors, held open by two rather stern-looking men. The fragrance of lavender and marguerites filled her nostrils, reminding her of long, lazy summers spent playing in the grass, trying to outrun Marina and Felipe before they turned into red-horned seals or oceanic trolls or whichever strange creature her imagination had cooked up. Her legs itched with the urge to run now, but her high-heeled shoes and Madre's grip were simply too tight.

Candles shone from the giant chandelier above, casting shadows across the polished marble floors and outlining the sneers which oozed from the family portraits. Anxiety balled in her stomach. Even the pictures knew she was out of place.

'Stand up straight,' Madre hissed in her ear. 'Hasn't Señora Tenso taught you anything about posture?'

Tiggy could almost feel the weight of five books pressing down on her head, almost hear her governess's voice yapping about becoming a gliding swan. She forced her body upright, even as sweat beaded down her neck, turning the peach of her dress a dark, rusted orange.

A butler took their coats and ushered them through a grand archway.

Her breath froze in her lungs. The ballroom was grand, with a domed ceiling and curved walls, bigger than her entire house. But it wasn't the size which threw her; it was the lack of colour. But for the array of vibrant masks, everything was muted. The cream of the marble floors, the pastel blue of the walls, the soft flicker of candlelight and the crisp white blouses of the men. Worst of all, every woman waltzing upon the gleaming dance floor seemed to be wearing cream. She most definitely was not a gliding swan. Indeed, she was a canary amongst a sea of gliding swans and, to make matters worse, it was as though she'd walked into the room and screamed – even though her mouth was dry and her throat had closed – because everybody beneath that domed ceiling stopped what they were doing and stared.

Padre leant into her, his breath warm and reassuring against her cheek. 'It's because you look so lovely.'

Eventually, people returned to their conversations, their waltzing and drinking, and the Governor approached them, his arms outstretched. He had a round face which gleamed as though he had just finished a leg of goat and rubbed the oil into his skin, and wore an eye mask which Tiggy assumed was meant to be a shark, though the jewelled teeth which lined the underside were square rather than pointed. *Definitely more horse than shark*, she thought.

'The family de Fortune, welcome, welcome.' He exchanged a salute with Padre and kissed Madre lightly on each cheek.

Madre smiled her sweetest smile and brushed a strand of mermaid hair behind her ear. 'What a spectacular way to begin the Bloodmoon celebrations.'

'Indeed,' the Governor replied. 'Far more civilized than the beach carnival the harbour heathens have planned for Bloodmoon Day. I swear we won't be able to see the Bloodmoon, the amount of fireworks they're planning to release.'

'I can't wait,' Tiggy whispered before she could stop herself.

The Governor looked her up and down as though noticing her for the first time. 'Well, well. You have turned into quite the young lady, haven't you, Antigua. I don't think you could look less like a Sea Golem if you tried.'

Tiggy repositioned her mask, suddenly very grateful it hid half of her face. She hated being inspected, especially by men who were used to getting what they wanted.

'I know Salvador is dying to see you,' the Governor

continued, oblivious to her discomfort. He gestured towards a primped young man at the other side of the room, who leant against a chair as he held court with a group of girls in an over-loud voice. The women rewarded him with the occasional trill of fake laughter. Tiggy prickled at the sight of him, her stomach immediately contracting as though she'd eaten a mouldy fig.

Before she could protest, the Governor was guiding her away from her parents and towards his son. 'Salvador, look who has arrived.'

Salvador turned, annoyance at being interrupted clearly logged on his face. His mask was pushed on to his head, revealing a groomed brow and two dark eyes which never stopped scanning the room for approval. He looked at Tiggy, his thin moustache twitching as his features decided which expression to settle on. Eventually, he adopted a simpering look, plucking Tiggy's hand from her side and planting a kiss on her knuckles. His lips felt wet and unsavoury. Tiggy forced herself to curtsey, convinced that her knees would creak loudly in objection. And without a word, without even asking her, Salvador clasped her round the waist and shoved her on to the dance floor.

Tiggy felt her back grow rigid like a plank, the desire to shake his hands away almost overwhelming, but when her parents' faces flashed by – proud, happy – she forced her feet to move in time to the music. Even making an effort, dancing with Salvador was harder than she'd imagined. She'd been taught the dances of the Haven gentry by Padre, who always let her lead and didn't mind when she stood on his toes. Salvador, however, seemed to push and pull her wherever he pleased, bundling her along so she felt like a marionette bending to her master's will. She could feel her supper nipping at the base of her throat.

'Antigua,' he said, breathless from all the shoving, blinking the sweat from his lizard eyes, 'it is always a pleasure.'

She nodded, afraid that if she spoke her words would betray her, causing a deafening *GET YOUR HANDS OFF ME* to ricochet around the walls. Seemingly unaware of her discomfort, he proceeded to jostle her across the dance floor, glancing sideways to check he had an audience. 'I'm not convinced by the mask, but your dress is simply divine. So colourful.'

Tiggy forced out her voice. 'Madre designed it herself.'

He nodded. 'Yes. I suspected as much.'

'What do you mean?'

'Well, peach . . . it was fashionable *last* year, I believe.'

Tiggy felt her cheeks heat. She opened her mouth to reply, but Salvador seemed to enjoy talking as much as he enjoyed pushing her around the dance floor. 'And will you dress as a Sea Golem tomorrow night? I bet you'll get loads of treats if you do. Funny how even now, everyone's so scared of Golems. You know, it's probably all a myth.'

'Don't let the townsfolk hear you say that. It was their boys who were stolen. It may have been hundreds of years ago, but time doesn't heal all scars.'

Salvador smirked. 'I don't dispute that the boys were stolen. I merely dispute their fate. I mean, *Golems*? Seriously? The idea of a mage turning an army of boys into his puppets is simply ludicrous. How could one man force another to act against their will?'

Tiggy felt his hands tug at her waist, forcing her to sidestep to the right in time to the beat. 'You're doing a pretty good job yourself,' she muttered under her breath.

Suddenly the tempo increased, causing Salvador

to twirl her in a circle. The heeled shoes pinched her toes and seemed to slip against the polished floor; her feet tangled with his and she tumbled downwards in a whoosh of peach fabric, pain shooting up her tail bone as she clattered through a series of chairs and people. The screech of violins and rumble of falling cellos told her before she even whacked the floor that she'd somehow managed to land amongst the string quartet.

She sat amongst the carnage, blinking quickly. Beyond the complaints of the musicians, the upturned chairs and the strewn violin bows, through the smog of humiliation and the ache in her behind, she could see an entire ballroom of masked gentry gawking.

Salvador glared down at her, his face all puffy and his moustache twitching. He didn't even offer her his hand, instead lowering his mask as if to hide from the onlookers. The golden papier mâché tentacles of an octopus shone with more jewels than Tiggy had ever seen. *Great, now he has even more hands*, she thought to herself.

'How embarrassing,' he hissed. 'I can't believe I ever liked you. You belong on the pier, selling fish, not in a ballroom.'

Mortification grabbed hold of Tiggy's heart, forcing it to pump even more red-hot blood to her neck and face. She scrabbled back to a sitting position, avoiding the eyes of the horrified musicians as they rescued their instruments from the floor.

Padre was beside her in a shot, deftly picking his way between the musicians and hooking his hands beneath her arms. He helped her wobble into an upright position and led her away from the quartet. 'Come now,' he whispered in his soothing tone. 'It doesn't matter that you fall. What matters is you stand again.'

Salvador brushed down his trousers as though he could brush away the shame. 'Did nobody teach you to dance?'

She caught Salvador's accusatory eye – two dark pits sunk into the gleaming mass of jewels. 'Yes, of course I've learnt to dance,' she managed to squeak. 'But Padre always let me lead.'

Salvador laughed. 'Lead? Don't you know that you're a girl?'

Anger slammed into Tiggy, eclipsing any humiliation and forcing her fists to clench and her legs to shake. 'And?' Her voice emerged sharp and thorn-like, causing a disapproving whisper to breeze through the crowd.

'Antigua,' Madre warned.

'And . . .' Salvador sputtered, 'you're supposed to let the man lead.'

Tiggy ignored Madre, and that nagging voice in her head which told her to at least try and fit in. 'Look, I didn't even want to dance with you, you just grabbed me.'

His face displayed utter confusion. 'But, but . . . you're supposed to *want* to dance with me.'

She stepped up to him, her nostrils flaring. 'I met two maggots today I would rather have danced with.'

The gasp of the crowd was overshadowed only by Madre's cry of disappointment.

Tiggy felt a hundred eyes boring into her back – she would surely break from the weight of the disgrace. She wished her mask would grow and grow until it became a mighty shield, hiding her completely. So before the humiliation leaked from her eyes, belying her strong, fierce expression, she hitched up her skirt, kicked off her heels and stormed from the ball.

CHAPTER 4

She streaked across the driveway, feet burning from the bite of pebbles, eyes hot with tears. Stupid dress, stupid ball, stupid, stupid Salvador. She reached the peak of the hill, the wind on her face and the sun finally dissolving into the horizon.

'Antigua.' The voice was sharper than the pain in her chest, causing her head to whip around.

Madre stomped towards her, thunder in her face and mask in her hand. 'What on earth were you thinking? Salvador will never want you now.'

Tiggy stamped her foot, suddenly feeling more

like an angry toddler than a young woman. 'Good. My sole mission in life is not to be desired by a slime-ball like Salvador.'

'Then what is it?' Madre's pretty face was scrunched with frustration. 'What is your goal?'

'I don't know yet. But it certainly isn't to swan around a manor house for the rest of my life. I couldn't bear it.'

Madre stepped towards her, determination forcing her voice into a low whisper. 'Antigua de Fortune, you are the daughter of an officer, the daughter of a lady. Your padre and I, we have worked so hard, made such sacrifices, to provide you and Diego with a good life. When will you realize you can't spend your days running around the harbour pretending to be a pirate? It's time to grow up.'

Something dark and nameless grew inside Tiggy's gut, a mixture of anger, defiance and injustice. It pushed into her ribcage, up her throat and spilt out of her mouth before she could stop it. 'I never asked you to make any sacrifices. What if I *have* grown up? What if this is who I am?'

Madre clasped her hands to her head. 'Oh, Antigua, I just want what is best for you. Please, *please*, will you just be the daughter we raised you to be.'

'Madre, you're not listening.' Tiggy jabbed a finger to her heart. 'What if I *can't* be? What if this *is* me?'

'Well then, you can just, just . . . change.'

Change. The word was a bullet. It blasted through the anger, shattering it into a million pieces so that it floated like ashes around Tiggy's feet. An over-whelming sadness settled inside her. She blinked at her mother for a moment, trying to pull some sense from the rejection, trying to see the madre who had rocked her to sleep when she was little. But all she could see was a hard-faced woman who wanted her to change. Tiggy longed to tell Madre how hurt she felt, how *trapped* she felt, yet words suddenly seemed useless – nothing more than a string of random grunts and pauses to hurl at each other. So instead, she turned and ran down the hill, stubbing her toes on clumps of dried grass, cursing her bootless feet.

Madre's voice chased her like a pack of hungry dogs. 'Tiggy, where are you going? It isn't safe on your own at night.'

Tiggy ran until Madre's voice vanished completely, until the palm trees began to sprout and her feet were surely running on upturned needles. She reached the beach a sweating, heaving mass of sorrow and, with her vision so blurred with tears, she didn't spot the approaching rock pool or the pesky tangle of seaweed, which snarled around her ankles and caused her to face-plant into the water below.

Quickly, the pool closed around her head, filling her nostrils and her ears, pushing its salty fingers beneath her mask and into her eyes, causing them to sting and shrink in their sockets. Her hearing muffled, her lungs froze, and she knew she should heave her face from the cold, briny pool. Yet something held her there.

A sense of belonging, of familiarity.

And it was there, cradled by the waters, a far-off voice found her. It was the voice of a young woman, a scream which gurgled and turned as though reaching through gallons and gallons of saltwater.

Help me, the voice called. *Help me, please.*

CHAPTER 5

Clara stretched out her arms, muttering under her breath as her hands bumped against the glass edges of her tank. A chain of bubbles zigzagged from her lips towards the murky surface of the water. What she wouldn't give to be able to move freely, to dive towards the ocean floor and snake between shafts of sunlight, to hear the call and click of the orca whales and to feel the currents nudge against her skin. Her long tail trembled, iridescent patches beginning to sparkle beneath its violet scales in anticipation of a bottomless sea. *Not today*, she told it sadly.

The creak of a wooden plank pulled her from her thoughts. Her heart accelerated in her chest as she struggled to focus through the salt water, thick with seaweed and flecks of sand. She squinted, causing the lines of the wooden cabin to sharpen. Between the chests of coins, exotic carved plates and the taxidermy of exotic land creatures, most of which Clara had never before seen, a silhouette walked towards her – swiftly, purposefully, as though flaunting its freedom. The figure gained clarity the closer it came and the candles around her tank caused shadows to twist across his fitted jacket and tricorn hat. There was no mistaking that he was a pirate, though he looked different from the ones who had captured her . . . neater, better dressed. He looked like a gentleman, the buttons of his waistcoat polished till they glowed, but she could tell from the cruel slant of his brow that he was anything but.

He carried a bucket in his right hand and she could sense the fish moving inside its thin metal walls, even from her tank. Her stomach awakened. He stopped an arm's length away and clanged the bucket down beside his leather boots, sending the fish darting this way and that. This close, she could see that his face was carved from cruelty, whittled into a series of angles and frowns which could be described as handsome, if only his eyes didn't possess the promise of blood. Clara realized she was holding the water in her gills – three slashes on either side of her chest. Too afraid to even breathe.

He pushed his nose against the pane so that two circles of mist formed above his mouth, and his dark eyes seemed to cut through the water straight into her soul. She shivered. The seaweed swirled around her, the waters responding immediately to her distress. Instinctively, she pushed her palms against the tank so she could block out his hateful face.

'You must be hungry.' His voice was so deep it sent vibrations through the glass directly into her palms.

She recoiled, wishing she appeared braver, more defiant. So she shook her head, even though she'd spent most of the day imagining sinking her teeth into entire shoals of whiting.

The pirate smiled. His teeth were yellow and speckled with food, and his fingers toyed with a glass vial which hung from his neck. 'Really? My men told me you haven't eaten anything in two days. I don't want you starving to death now – not when it's taken so long to find another one of you loathsome creatures.'

Anger reared inside her. How dare he call her loathsome. And he hadn't found her, he had *stolen* her. Wrenched her from the ocean, from her darling family. She began to beat her fists against the transparent barrier, a string of curses leaving her mouth in a flurry of bubbles. As the water spiralled faster and faster, it lifted her dark hair around her face and caused her to vanish inside a cloud of silt.

The man ignored her outcries and stood on a rickety, wooden stool. He poised the bucket above his head so he could empty the contents into the vat. She stilled. Her great tail flicked wildly beneath her, catching in the candle glow like a violet sheet of gossamer. She tipped her face towards the surface. At least now she could eat.

'I figured you'd refuse,' the pirate said. 'Merfolk are notoriously stubborn.' He slopped the fish into the salt water below.

Only they weren't fish.

Dark ribbons floated downwards, before jolting back to life and slithering around her flesh. Eels. And judging from the look of them, the kind which deliver an agonizing shock if touched. Panic exploded in her chest. Yet her mother's voice found her, calm and laced with warmth. *It is OK, my little starfish, they will not harm you.* Clara ordered her heart to slow and her gills to gently suck the sea water. *Never fear the fruits of the sea, my love.* Finally, when the anxiety had melted away, Clara spoke. Her voice gurgled through the water and rang around the dark, wooden cabin like a bell. 'You have forgotten that they will not harm me, pirate. Eels, merfolk . . . we spring from the same sea.' She looked upwards and addressed the dark strips of danger directly, quoting the guardian merfolk hex. A smile clutched at her lips – these words had been known to tame even the most ferocious of great whites.

'*Children of the ocean, hear me and be calmed . . .*'

But the man interrupted her, his voice twisting the hex into something mocking and hard. '*For I am your protector, and never shall be harmed.*' His laughter filled the cabin. 'Did you really think your silly rhymes could protect you against *me*?' His eyes narrowed, growing darker than the eels themselves. Then he pressed his hands together as though in prayer. A ball of turquoise light formed between his palms – buzzing, crackling, illuminating the underbelly of his stubbled chin.

Clara began to tremble. Her tail quivered, as though dipped in the freezing waters of the Atlantic. *What is this dark magic?* she thought.

The man glared at her with venomous eyes and his pointed finger began to trace a pattern before him, a trail of turquoise light glimmering in its wake. Within seconds, the gaunt outline of a dagger sizzled in the gloom like the strangest of lightning shows. Clara watched, transfixed, as the point of the blade rotated to face her.

'*Attarque,*' the man whispered, shooting his palms towards her.

The blade followed the direction of his fingers, rushing towards her and dissolving in a crack of blue mist against the wall of the tank. Clara screamed, watching in horror as the strange fog rippled through her tank like a wave of bioluminescent algae. Within seconds, the light reached the eels, and they pulled their spindly bodies into taut, black arrows.

Every one of them pointed at her.

'Now,' the mage said, 'may I suggest you tell me what I need to know?'

She stared at him, feeling more lost than anyone should when floating in a tank the size of a rock pool. 'What?'

The mage smiled, long and slow. 'I need you to tell me the prophecy of the Bloodmoon.'

Clara lay on the bottom of her tank, running her hands across her tailfins and checking for rips. The mage had called off the eels a while ago, and they now happily zipped above her head, completely unaware of the damage they'd just caused.

She swallowed down another wave of tears and focused on healing her fins. She found another rip, and with nimble fingers pressed the pieces of skin together; the tiniest of blue sparks flashed beneath her fingertips and seeped into the surrounding water like drops of ink. The rip sealed. The magic of the ocean ran through her fingers; it was in the veins of all the merfolk, and they were supposed to use it to help and heal. Never before had she seen the turquoise light of the sea wielded with such force, such brutality, as in the hands of the mage.

She had heard stories about the Pirate King, everyone had, but he was long dead. And the turquoise of magic, brandished outside of the water, looked more like lightning – jagged and fierce. Surely the mage had stolen the soft inky magic she had come to love and moulded it into something hateful. A weapon. She shuddered, returning to her poor, injured tail.

That was when she felt it. A surge of something unpleasant in the pit of her stomach – a feeling like she was being watched, laughed at . . . ridiculed. She glanced around her. But only the wood of the cabin and a selection of stolen treasures lay outside the glass panes of her tank. There wasn't even a window that someone could peek through, for she was sunk deep into the belly of the ship, away from the prying eyes of the crew and any passing merfolk.

She tried to shrug the feeling away. Maybe it was the lifeless stare of all the stuffed animals which surrounded her tank. Or maybe it was guilt playing tricks on her: the guilt of finally telling the mage what he'd wanted to know. She looked up at the eels and whispered in a sad voice, 'I know it isn't your fault, little ones.'

The mage had tortured her until her frail body could no longer cope and the secrets had burst from her lips without permission. She shook her head angrily. *I should have been stronger. Now that the mage knows the prophecy of the Bloodmoon, there will be no stopping him.*

That feeling of being watched grew in her

stomach again. Yet now it was growing, shifting, turning into anger and rage. She could hear a voice – somebody telling her that she needed to change.

Change. The word seemed to hit her like a harpoon in the chest. She squeezed her eyes shut and a face swam into her mind's eye. A girl, about her age, stood in front of a grand building, just like the ones Clara had seen in the distance when she had once dared to surface near the Fortune Isles. The girl had light brown skin, curly black hair piled on top of her head against its will, and wore a strange Golem mask, built from seaweed and barnacles.

Clara's eyes flew open. A vision. Was she linking to a human? She thought back to the image. Yes, the girl was wearing a dress: she had . . . *legs*. Clara shook her head in disbelief. Everyone knew it was impossible for merfolk to link to land walkers. Indeed, even linking with other children of the sea was rare, only occurring at times of grave danger. *Well*, Clara thought bitterly, *I am indeed in grave danger, and beggars can't be choosers. Perhaps this land-girl can help.*

She focused again on the image of the girl, who now ran down a hill, slipping on the soil and bumping into shrubs. Clara could feel the stinging in her tailfins as though she herself was running with bare feet. She didn't know who this girl was, or even where she was, but she knew one thing for sure – the girl was her best chance of getting out of this hateful tank.

Gathering every last morsel of strength into her throat, Clara roared at the top of her voice, 'Help me, help me, please.'

Nothing. The girl carried on running, bursting on to the beach, utterly oblivious to Clara's distress. The link wasn't strong enough. If only the girl would enter the sea, feel the water consume her, let the salt become part of her soul . . . maybe then the link would grow and Clara could reach out to her. But everyone knew that humans didn't dare swim in the ocean, not since the Pirate King turned the ocean creatures against them all those years ago.

It was useless. The girl was a land-liver; she had legs for goodness sake. It was a miracle Clara could even see her, let alone reach out to her. Clara could feel the heat of frustration growing behind her eyes, yet still she focused helplessly on the girl in the vision. As if in response to Clara's desperation, a jumble of seaweed clung to the girl's foot, toppling her head first into a small rock pool.

Clara gasped.

The salty water in her tank seemed to choke the breath from her body. Her gills no longer worked. Frantically, she ran her fingers beneath her armpits and felt the three long openings with a tremor of relief. Her gills hadn't vanished; she was simply feeling what the girl was feeling, submerged in water and deprived of air.

The link was strong. Clara knew that now was her chance, so once again she roared at the top of her voice: 'Help me, help me, please.'

And, as if by magic, the girl heaved her head from the water, searching the air for a disembodied voice.

CHAPTER 6

Soaked to the bone with water and sadness, Tiggy flopped beside the rock pool. Had she simply imagined the voice? Had the strain of the evening become too much? She pulled down her Golem mask so it hung around her neck like a grisly piece of jewellery and turned her mind back to the ball and Salvador, back to Madre's cruel, cruel words. She thought perhaps she could still hear them, as if they'd been imprinted on her brain, an echo of sadness: *will you just be the daughter you ought to be?*

Her eyes misted with tears and she looked across

the sea; stars broke upon its surface as it churned rhythmically towards the sand. She was at the very edge of the island now, the very edge of Haven. It would be so easy just to swim away.

Something in her peripheral vision caught her eye. A drunken sailor – with long dark hair and a look of determination embedded into her sleeping face – lay unconscious in the sands. The woman was too close to the shore and would no doubt drown if the clutches of the liquor were stronger than the sting of the sea when it reached her face, so without further thought Tiggy stumbled across the sand and began to drag her inland, towards the palms where the ocean never quite reaches.

Something metal glinted on the beach next to the sailor. Curiously, she sifted the grains of sand from its silver form. It was a silver cylinder which fitted perfectly in Tiggy's palm, and poised on top, between an intricate mesh of metal lacework, was a crystal the size of a marble. She ran her fingers across it, stopping only when a little nub disturbed the smoothness. She pressed down. *Click*. A small blade unfolded and Tiggy realized she was holding a knife.

She gazed at it for a moment. She didn't like knives – was wary of the damage they could inflict –

but the polished blade held her reflection like a mirror, and she studied her face as she might a stranger's. Same eyes, same lips, same nose – yet tonight she looked alien. It was her hair. Piled on top of her head as if she were a princess. She tugged the clips loose, allowing her curls to tumble freely down her back, and then re-examined herself in the thin sheet of metal. Better. Yet Madre's voice continued to beat around her head like a flock of vicious birds, drowning out the roar of the waves and the snuffling of the sailor below. *Change. Change. Change.* But her own voice snapped back, fuelled with that familiar sense of anger and unfairness. 'You want me to change?' she asked the knife. 'Well then, I will change.'

She reached behind her neck and pulled her hair so it formed a tight, black cord. Then, with skilful hands she twisted the blade and positioned it against the base of her neck. In one swift motion, she sliced the cord clean from her head, her hand falling towards her and scattering long, dark feathers across the sand. She felt weightless, free. She ruffled her fingers through her short crop of curls and laughed. 'Is this what you wanted, Madre?'

Silence.

She had expected some sort of response, if not from the drunken sailor, then perhaps from the island itself. But the waves continued to roll, the stars continued to blink and the soft swish of the palm leaves continued to tint the wind. 'Stupid island,' she muttered, before absent-mindedly pocketing the small dagger.

She looked towards the port. It seemed to beckon – the glint of the candles in the windows, the sound of pianos and laughter weaving through the night air. At least she could show Marina and Felipe her new hair. At least they would tell her that Madre was a big-eared bat and of course Tiggy didn't need to change.

The Signum tavern was a pocket of activity. Men slopping ale down their front, singing out of key and bickering across tables, the air heavy with rum, fish and damp wood, oil lamps throwing out their warm, orange glow. The swish of the string quartet felt so very far away right now, like another world.

Tiggy knew she looked a state, with her ripped ballgown, soaking hair and bare feet, but nobody turned to look – although she didn't exactly fit in, she didn't stand out either, for this was a place you couldn't stand out, not when there were men with sea clay dried to their faces.

Gabriella looked up from the bar, rum still pouring into a glass below. She had Felipe's strong nose and Marina's wide-set eyes. It was hard to imagine her as a seal. She glanced at Tiggy, and at first her face was completely devoid of recognition, then, after a second it dawned on her that the dishevelled young rat was in fact her daughter's best friend. 'Tiggy!' she exclaimed. 'Shouldn't you be at the Golem Ball?'

Tiggy slumped on to a bar stool. 'I would rather be eaten alive by a swarm of Golems.'

'Golems did a lot of things, but as far I'm aware, they never ate anyone.' Without a downwards glance, Gabriella stopped pouring just before the liquor overflowed. She slammed the bottle down on the bar, slopping amber liquid on to the wood.

'Well, that's me out of luck then, isn't it?' Tiggy ordered her eyes to remain dry and her bottom lip not to tremble.

'That bad, huh?' Gabriella said.

'Worse than bad.'

Gabriella squeezed her hand. 'Come now. You live in Haven, the heart of the Fortune Isles, the soul of the ocean . . . the centre of the world. *Nothing* here can ever be worse than bad.'

The kindness caused the sadness to multiply, layering inside Tiggy until she felt she might explode in a wave of tears. She swallowed the feeling down, even though her throat was spiked like coral.

'Hey,' Gabriella said, clearly trying to change the subject. 'Love your new locks. Much more practical.'

Tiggy had somehow forgotten about her hair. She ran her fingers through it, marvelling at how quickly they met the air. 'Thanks. I was told I needed to change, and so I did.'

'Bah, who told you that? One of your father's foolish comrades up at the manor?'

Tiggy nodded, the truth burning her throat. 'Yeah.' She glanced around, afraid the lie would surface on her face. 'Is Marina here? Felipe?'

Gabriella nodded. 'They're in bed. I'm sure they won't mind if you wake them though.'

'Thanks.' As Tiggy slipped from her bar stool, a large man approached her. He looked as though he was built from wax; his ear lobes dangled unnaturally low and his nose was pitted and bulbous like the top of a well-used candle. He adjusted an eyepatch as though trying to get a better look at Tiggy.

'Hey, you're Señor de Fortune's daughter, aren't

you?' He part gargled, part spoke, as though ale were still stuck in his throat.

Tiggy nodded, holding her breath to avoid his stench – ale, cigars and raw fish.

He studied her with his single eye. 'I knew your madre before you were born. Owes me an eye, she does.'

Tiggy's interest piqued. '*My* madre? Are you sure?'

He opened his mouth to reply, but Gabriella leant across the bar. 'Hey, Benito, fancy a rum on the house?'

Benito turned towards the offer, revealing a patch of red, crinkly skin where his hair should have been. Tiggy winced. It looked as if he had been partially scalped. How did this man, who seemed to have lived a life of salt water and swords rather than tea parties and frocks, know Madre? And surely the eye comment was no more than a joke. Without thought, she gripped his shoulder, trying to draw him back to the conversation.

But Gabriella looked at him long and hard, her fingers brushing against the silver winkle shell which hung from her delicate neck. Was it Tiggy's imagination, or did that necklace flash a vibrant blue, as though it held the magic of the oceans inside its tiny metal cone?

Benito shrugged Tiggy's hand away, lifting the rum to his cracked lips. 'Sorry, lass. My memory's not so good these days.'

Tiggy glared at Gabriella, who simply smiled. 'Why don't you go see Marina and Felipe?'

Frustration yanked at Tiggy's stomach – it was becoming an all-too-familiar sensation, she decided. An argument started to form on her tongue. She would find out how this man knew Madre if it killed her, but before she could even draw breath, a wail from outside cut through the air like nothing she had ever heard before. Deep, guttural, like an animal being slaughtered. The panes in the tavern windows shook and Benito dropped his rum in shock, his glass bouncing off the bar and shattering on the boards below.

Tiggy bolted to the front door, curiosity pulling at her legs and making her movements sharp and quick. She ignored Gabriella's warning cry and stepped into the salt-coated night, a mass of drunken sailors piling out behind her.

Beyond the pier, where she and Felipe had sat only that afternoon, where Diego had mounded his stones, a dark shape rose from the waves.

'Is that a galleon?' she asked.

But she already knew the answer. It was too big to be a galleon. As it moved closer, crashing into the pier and dragging it into the water as though it were no more than a strip of paper, she realized that it was a sea creature of some kind. She could make out the sheen of its skin, the rounded top of its monstrous head. She looked in horror as black fleshy snakes, bigger than the trunk of any phoenix palm, lifted from the water and writhed through the air. The underbelly of the snakes glinted pale in the moonlight, revealing a set of suckers larger than serving platters. *Not snakes*, Tiggy thought, fear wringing the sweat from her body, *tentacles*.

'It's a squid,' she shrieked.

Panic broke out around her – sailors darting back into the tavern, soldiers loading rifles and buccaneers dashing to save their beloved boats. The sound of the warning bell filled the air like an angry bird. *Clang. Clang. Clang.* And, as if in response, the squid released another wail. This time, Tiggy felt it in her feet. A breeze hit her face, and she was sure she could smell the stench of its breath, a combination of fish and decay. Yet in spite of the commotion and the terror which crushed her chest, she remained completely still, watching with a mixture of fascination and horror as the creature reached the harbour.

She had heard tales of giant squids, but never seen one. They were supposed to be peaceful creatures, preferring deeper, cooler waters and avoiding the shallows of the Isles. But this squid did not look peaceful at all. As it reared from the water, searching for food, its tentacles opened like a horrific bloom, revealing a giant grey beak at their centre. Tiggy already knew that squids had beaks instead of mouths, but never before had she seen one so huge, one that could surely crush a galleon with a single snap. Whirring towards them, the tentacles flailed madly, smashing through boats the size of houses, sea foam and shards of wood firing into the air like shrapnel. Yet there was something strange about the squid's eyes: a bright turquoise light fizzed across them.

The creature reached the port and stopped, its giant body rising from the shallows like a dark, glossy shipwreck. Its tentacles calmed, and Tiggy risked snatching a breath. The bell continued to clang. She noticed for the first time that soldiers raced towards the pier, their weapons aimed.

'No,' she cried helplessly into the dark. 'Look at

its eyes. I think it may be enchanted, you can't just kill it.'

The soldiers now lined the beach, rigging up the cannons and arming their guns. Something went off inside Tiggy like a flare. She began to run towards the soldiers, pumping her legs as fast as they would carry her. The boom of a cannon made her heart leap against her ribcage, pulling her to an abrupt halt. Were they firing on the squid? But an explosion of sand beside the soldiers answered her question in an instant. She looked towards the source of the cannonball, across the dark waters and towards the star-slung horizon – a fleet of ships emerged from the dimness, masts impaling the clouds and sails cracking in the wind. Waves kicked and sputtered at their great bows as if even the sea was afraid.

Fear wound around Tiggy's chest, squeezing all the breath from her body. 'Pirates,' she gasped. 'An army of pirates.'

Benito – the man she had met in the bar – stomped up behind and stopped by her side. 'Them be more than just pirates, Señorita de Fortune.'

Very slowly, the giant squid which seemed to lead the fleet of ships parted its tentacles and opened its jagged beak in a great yawn.

Tiggy blinked, disbelief clouding her vision.

Standing upon its tongue was the outline of a man. A turquoise light crackled between his hands, lighting up the inside of the creature's cave-like jaws. *A mage.* She had heard tales of sorcerers of the waves, of course she had, but their powers didn't extend any further than simple hexes to heal injured sea creatures or help guide ships home . . . Surely the turquoise glow was nothing more than a fancy parlour trick. And yet there he was, standing on the tongue of a giant squid. *A giant squid.* Anything seemed possible right now.

A gang of pirates stood on the tongue behind the mage, illuminated by his sea-green glow. Every one of them carried weapons and death in their hands.

And just before the cannonballs flew, just before the rifles erupted and the army of pirates stormed the beach, Tiggy watched as the mage drew together the turquoise light to form the spiky shape of a rifle, thrust his hands forwards so that the shape dissolved into a cloud of blue, and mouthed one single word: *Attarque.*

CHAPTER 7

The pirates raced on to the beach, knives raised, pistols drawn, battle cries falling from their mouths. The soldiers fired with ferocity, and yet each bullet seemed to dissolve in a turquoise mist before reaching its target. And any soldiers foolish enough to venture into the waters were instantly picked off by sharks. Tiggy knew she should run, yet she was paralysed with both dread and awe, unable to pull her eyes from the dark magic unfolding before her.

Something landed on her shoulder. She gasped,

her brain on high alert, and the sensation unlocked her body. She spun quickly, raising her hands and imagining an attacker armed with turquoise light. But it was Lucia, her usually relaxed face pulled taut.

'Tiggy, it isn't safe here.' Her voice sounded in bursts between the warning bell and cannon fire. 'You need to get home, back to the hills. The pirates never make it past the port.'

Tiggy nodded, though she feared this was no ordinary raid. 'What about you? Come with me.'

Lucia pulled a curved knife from her belt and released a smile which never quite reached her eyes. 'And miss out on all the fun? Not a chance.'

Benito grinned, the spark of adventure lending his worn face a renewed youth. 'You said it.'

'Wait,' Tiggy called, but they had already gone, racing towards the harbour with their blades drawn.

Feeling very alone, Tiggy turned and bumped straight into Gabriella.

'*Vivar mar,*' Gabriella whispered, thanking the Kraken. 'Quick, into the tavern. You'll be safe there.'

Fear had overshadowed the memory of the ball, and all Tiggy wanted now were her parents and brother. The safety of home. 'Lucia said it was safer away from the port. We could get Marina and Felipe and hide at my house . . . ?'

But Gabriella was already guiding her towards the tavern entrance with surprisingly strong hands. 'Those pirates are no ordinary pirates, Antigua. The safest place is the home of a selkie, trust me.' It was the first time Gabriella had ever confessed her selkie roots. And as Tiggy passed through the door of the tavern, she was sure that a strange conical shape glowed turquoise from its wooden planks – slightly wonky, slapdash even, as though drawn in a hurry but, without doubt, a winkle shell.

'It's for protection,' Gabriella hissed. 'Just keep moving.'

'What do you mean, no ordinary pirates?' Tiggy asked.

But Gabriella didn't reply, too intent on closing the door firmly behind her.

If Tiggy had thought the tavern was full before the arrival of the squid, it was ready to burst now. It seemed that every man and woman without a sword knew of Gabriella's protective powers. The cry of hungry babies and tired children mixed with the clang of swords and crack of bullets outside. Tiggy shuddered. It was so strange, so *unnatural*, to hear such innocence so tightly stitched with the sounds of death. She scanned the cowering families, seeking out Felipe and Marina and, when she could not find them, she rushed towards the back of the house where they both slept.

She reached the stairs only to see her friends stumble from their bedroom door, their faces blurry with sleep and confusion. Felipe had unscrewed his wooden leg as part of his bedtime routine, and so, hopping slightly, clung to the bannister to prevent himself toppling.

'What's going on?' Marina asked. She looked different from usual, altered by sleep; her long, black hair stuck from her head as though she'd stood in a gale, her big brown eyes seemed to have shrunk as she squinted against the candle in her hand, and an oversized, pink nightgown almost entirely hid her bronze skin.

'Quick,' Tiggy said, hitching up her frock and taking the stairs two at a time. 'I'll show you from the window.'

She dragged them both back into their room and jumped on to Marina's bed, which was pushed beneath the window sill. Felipe screwed in his wooden leg and blew out the freshly lit candles, plunging the room into a silvery, moon-brushed darkness. The three of them knelt side by side, faces pressed against the pane.

The sight below rekindled Tiggy's fear, her breath quickening in time with her friends'. The beach was littered with soldiers – injured or worse – and many pirates had already reached the port, where they forced their way into the nearby houses and taverns. The screams of children made her blood run cold.

'How did they get past the soldiers?' Marina gasped.

'There's some sort of dark magic at work,' Tiggy replied. 'Some of them arrived inside a giant squid.'

Felipe pulled his face from the window, his dark eyes filled with excitement. '*Inside* a giant squid? I've never heard of a mage with the power to control sea creatures before.'

'You should have seen the fancy light show he put on.' Tiggy looked beyond the port. The great galleons had already docked and a steady stream of pirates leapt from ropes into the water. 'And here comes his army,' she said, panic causing her words to slur.

Marina pointed to the street below, her voice emerging as an outraged squeak. 'They're taking the children!'

Tiggy's stomach spasmed as if she would vomit. Pirates normally left houses with sacks full of food and coins, not children, but Marina was right; slung over their broad shoulders, wriggling and squealing like pigs to the slaughter, were the children of Haven.

Tiggy squinted at the scene below. 'Not children, Marina. Boys. They're taking the *boys*.' Her fingers automatically grazed the Sea Golem mask, terror unfurling in her gut.

Felipe glanced at the disguise. 'It's just a story,' he said, even as the confidence wavered on his face. 'And even if it were true, the Pirate King was killed.'

'It's a heck of a coincidence though,' Marina said. 'In two days, it's the first Bloodmoon in fifty years.'

Tiggy and Felipe didn't reply; the idea of the curse reawakening was too horrific to contemplate. They watched in silence as desperate parents chased pirates down the street, tugging at shirts and pleading with no success.

Felipe leapt from the bed. The excitement in his eyes had been replaced by rage as he moved towards the door.

'Felipe,' Marina cried, 'where are you going?'

'I'm not going to stand by as someone takes our children.'

'I'll go with you,' Tiggy said, ashamed at how her voice faltered.

'No,' Marina clung to Tiggy's frock. 'It's safe in here – see how the pirates are avoiding our door.'

As though she'd been eavesdropping, Gabriella burst into the room. Slung across her arms was a long grey coat sewn from a fabric Tiggy had never before seen. Smooth, rubbery, glistening as though slightly damp. It looked almost like . . . *sealskin*. Before Tiggy could ask about the mysterious cloak, she was distracted by an even stranger sight. The necklace around Gabriella's neck had begun to burn with such intensity it hurt Tiggy's eyes. Gabriella glowered at her son, her usually dark eyes flashing a mysterious blue. 'And just where do you think you're going, Felipe?' She looked formidable, her face enveloped in a teal light, her expression fierce. Gone was the lovable barmaid who poured rum for a living. She was a warrior of the sea.

'They're stealing away the boys!' Felipe shouted, unaffected by his mother's glow.

'And what do you think *you* are, Felipe?'

'I'd like to see them try and take me,' Felipe whispered. 'I can fight now, Madre. I'm almost a man.'

Gabriella pulled herself taller, clutching the coat close to her chest. 'I know, dear-heart. But this is no ordinary attack, you'll be no match for the dark sorcery of the sea.'

'Has this got something to do with the curse of Haven?' Tiggy asked, the words sticking in her throat.

'I don't know,' Gabriella replied. 'All I know is that it's safest here. They've already reached the town. Soon they'll be in the hills.'

Something exploded inside Tiggy's stomach, blasting adrenalin through her veins and causing her heart to stammer in her chest. 'The hills?'

Gabriella looked at her, the realization of what she'd just said quickly translating into regret. 'Oh, Tiggy, I'm so sorry.'

But Tiggy could barely make out her words. Her ears rang, her head swirled and all she could think about was her little brother.

They were heading to the hills.

To her house.

His name left her lips in a single wisp: 'Diego.'

CHAPTER 8

Tiggy raced from the tavern, ducking round Gabriella's hands and ignoring the warnings of her friends. She ran faster than she'd ever run, her shoeless feet carrying her through the streets and houses, dodging pirates and soldiers, thoughts of Sea Golems and the Pirate King causing her throat to pulsate with dread.

The curse was lifted, the Pirate King killed . . . So why was this happening? Could history really be repeating itself? Marina was right: it couldn't be a coincidence that the boys were being stolen two days before the first Bloodmoon in fifty years. Her pace quickened. She had to reach her family before the pirates. The house had an attic above the servants' quarters, some disused outbuildings; it even had a secret basement – Diego could hide until the raid passed. The plan lit a fire in her belly, fuelling her body into a desperate sprint.

By the time she reached the base of the hills, her lungs threatened to collapse and her chest heaved so hard she felt she might burst. She glanced upwards, towards the jagged peaks of the mountains. Men and women in bandannas, carrying with them the stench of the sea, already wound their way up the paths, rifles and knives glinting beneath the moon.

She heard the beginnings of a storm – heavy rain, or perhaps even hail – yet the skies remained clear. 'What the—' she whispered as a swarm of spider crabs, each bigger than a large dog, scuttled after the pirates, followed by a couple of slower, even bigger, lobsters. Their eyes glowed with the same turquoise light as the giant squid. Were these creatures enchanted too? The sound of their legs hitting the path swelled like a drum roll, and Tiggy held her breath until they disappeared into the night.

She had to reach Diego, and quickly. The pirates

meant that the paths were unsafe, and she would be little use dead or kidnapped, so she would have to go the other way: through the palms and into the damp foliage of the hills. She glanced at her already bloodied feet, wishing desperately for her boots. Only then did she hear him, the rhythmic clunk of his wooden leg against the track. Felipe ran towards her, sweat pouring from his face. 'Thank goodness, you're OK.' He grabbed her hand. 'I just saw an army of giant crabs.'

'Me too. I think they're under the mage's enchantment. They had turquoise eyes, just like the squid.'

He blew out his cheeks in astonishment. 'Come on,' he said. 'We'd better hurry.'

His hand lay in hers like a warm stone, and Tiggy suddenly felt braver. Friends were definitely better than shoes, she decided. They wove between the palms like a needle pulling thread, and quickly made it to the higher, denser shrubs. The scent of brine faded, replaced by the intense-smelling moss and soil. Their muscles cramped and their throats burnt, yet they did not stop until they reached the pinnacle of the smallest hill.

Tiggy could make out her house against the black of the night. It's pale symmetrical face shone from the hill, candles transforming the windows into flickering eyes. The door was firmly closed. It looked peaceful. Safe.

'There's still time,' Tiggy whispered.

They glanced around them. Not a pirate in sight. They risked re-joining the path and ran towards the door. It was locked. Tiggy slammed her fists loudly against the wood, though she imagined the pulsing thump of her heart would be enough to rouse her parents.

Padre opened the door. 'Oh, Tiggy, thank goodness. I heard the alarm and was about to come looking for you. But you're safe now – the raids never reach the hills.'

Tiggy pushed past him. 'Where's Diego?' she screeched.

'It's late,' Padre said as he closed the door, confusion registering on his features. 'He's in bed.'

Madre rushed from the sitting room, her arms outstretched. The formality of her ballgown seemed strange when compared to the wild expression on her face. 'Antigua, you're home.' She clutched Tiggy to her chest, before holding her at arm's length, horror loosening her jaw. 'What have you done to your hair?'

Tiggy pushed Madre's hands away. 'It doesn't matter. We need to hide Diego right away.' She dashed through her parents, calling over her shoulder, 'There isn't time to explain.'

'Antigua,' Madre yelled. 'Get back here right now.'

But Tiggy was already vaulting the bannister and soaring up the stairs. 'Diego!' she called. 'Diego, wake up.'

She could hear Felipe's voice drifting upwards, telling her parents about the raid. She left them to it, bursting into her brother's room. It smelt so familiar, of snuffed-out wick and the tin of his little toy soldiers. She fell on to his sleeping form. 'Diego, Diego, you have to wake up.' She shook him vigorously, causing his quilt to slop to the ground.

He opened a sleepy eye. 'Tig?'

'Quickly,' she told him, pulling his legs from the bed and on to the floor. 'The pirates are coming. We need to hide.'

He swayed into a standing position, dreams attempting to pull him back down. 'Bobo,' he mumbled.

She grabbed the one-eyed bear from the pillow and shoved it into his arms. 'Yes, Bobo too.'

She slipped an arm around his slight shoulders

and steered him towards the door, yet his feet snagged on the carpet, his body still heavy with sleep. With an almighty grunt, Tiggy swept him into her arms and carried him from the room. He was far too big to carry, she decided, but needs must.

Padre was already on the landing. Lightly, he took Diego into his arms and trotted down the stairs, his usual casual step made urgent with fright. Tiggy watched with relief as her brother's dark lashes fluttered closed. With a little luck, he would sleep through the entire ordeal. She hoisted her skirt, hopped on the bannister and slid to the ground, beating Padre to the hall. Madre and Felipe were already in the kitchen, lifting the trapdoor to the cellar below, positioning the rug so it would flop back into place behind them. They were going to make it. It was going to be OK.

A loud clatter resounded throughout the hall. Tiggy reached towards the sleeping bundle in Padre's arms, horror sucking all the moisture from her mouth. The clatter sounded again. The door groaned in its frame, dust and wood fragments firing towards her.

'Quickly,' Padre said, bundling Diego into Tiggy's

arms and rushing to unlock the store cupboard and fetch his gun.

But it was too late.

Another clatter and the door flew inwards, revealing a slice of night and the biggest man Tiggy had ever seen. His braided grey hair fell like snakes around his shoulders and his narrow eyes drew every ounce of hope from her body. In his cigar-stained fingers was a dagger. Terror engulfed her, causing her breath to catch and her gut to contract. She backed away, pulling Diego to her body as though she could somehow hide him in the folds of her frock.

Diego stirred. 'Tig?' he whispered.

The pirate smiled, uncovering a set of broken teeth. 'Aren't you going to invite me in?' And without waiting for a response, he thundered into her home and ripped Tiggy's brother from her arms as though he were no more than a doll.

CHAPTER 9

Everything seemed to speed up. Tiggy was shouting, screaming, reaching for Diego; Felipe was running from the kitchen, brandishing a carving knife; Madre was close behind with a frying pan clutched in her hands; and Padre was dashing towards them, rifle poised. Relief filtered through Tiggy's body. Padre had his gun and he was the best shot in town.

The pirate with snake-hair backed away, clutching Diego across his body whilst the child bucked and reared in his arms. He eyed the weapon in Padre's hand with a gleeful sneer. 'What you gonna do, Señore? Shoot me through the boy?'

Padre faltered, his gun lowering, and this was all that was needed. Another monster of a man stepped from the shadows. This pirate was even bigger than the first, and his head – perched on top of his giant body – was topped with hair as white as snow, causing Tiggy to wonder if he was proof that mountains could exist in human form.

'Meet Brute,' Snake-hair said, gesturing to the man-mountain.

'Brute,' the giant grunted.

Padre lunged at Brute, burying his fist into the pirate's cheek. Padre was strong, highly trained, and the blow sounded like a rock thumping against earth. Tiggy expected the pirate to topple in an instant, yet Brute merely blinked and patted his brow as though a pesky drop of rain had landed on it. 'Brute?' he said, looking at Padre.

Before Padre could respond, Brute had clunked him over the head with the heel of his sword, causing him to crumple to the ground as though his bones had been stolen from his skin.

'Padre,' Tiggy gasped. Yet in spite of the panic which struck her heart, she didn't stoop to tend to her father, too afraid to take her eyes from Diego.

'Tiggy, help,' her brother cried.

She watched Diego's tiny hands rain blow upon blow on Snake-hair's broad chest. She gulped down the terror which threatened to consume her, and said in the strongest voice she could muster, 'Please, you don't have to do this.'

'The boss said to take the boys, so we're taking the boys,' Snake-hair said.

'What does the mage want with our boys?' she asked, desperate tears coursing down her face.

Snake-hair glanced at the mask which still hung from her neck. 'You'll find out soon enough, lassie.' Then both pirates turned and ran down the path. Diego reached over Snake-hair's shoulder and screamed, looking more terrified than Tiggy had ever seen before. She sprinted after them and jumped on Brute's back; he felt bigger than a horse and stank of liquor and unwashed hair, but Tiggy clung on as tight as she could, even as the pirate began ducking and weaving, swinging his blade so as to slice her from him.

Snake-hair paused and began to laugh. 'Attacked by a girl, hey?'

And within that moment, Madre and Felipe reached them, clutching their culinary weapons alongside their courage.

'There's another boy,' Snake-hair shouted, pointing to Felipe.

Powered by this new discovery, Brute gave an almighty shrug which sent Tiggy lurching to the ground. 'Brute,' he roared.

She landed with a thud, her head smacking the earth. Madre screamed, running at Brute with her frying pan raised, but the pirate simply turned his back so she bounced from him like a bluebottle against a glass pane, landing beside her daughter in a swirl of cream silk.

Tiggy groaned and tried to lever herself on to her elbows, but pain wrapped its serrated arms firmly around her body, pulling her back down to the soil. She heard the hail start up again. No. Not hail. The spider crabs and lobsters had arrived. The world began to fold in on itself: the stars blurred, the stink of liquor faded and the laughter of the pirates thinned in her ears. The last thing she saw before she blacked out was Brute tossing Felipe on to the back of a giant lobster, and a spider crab carrying her brother away, clutching him high above its head in two monstrous pincers as though he were no more than bait for fish.

The world beat in and out of focus. Tiggy could see the moon above, feel the ground below and smell the island at night. She raised her hands to her head, wincing with pain. Madre was leaning over her, tears plopping from her eyes and spotting Tiggy's face like rain.

'Diego?' Tiggy whispered, even though she knew the answer.

Madre released a sob in response.

Tiggy sat up too quickly and the world seemed to shift suddenly. It was as though her head was filled with sea water which slopped around when she moved.

'Steady,' Madre said, slipping a hand behind her daughter's back.

Tiggy noticed that some of the servants had woken with all the commotion. They stood around her in their nightgowns, tears sparkling on their cheeks.

'I'll carry her inside,' Antonio said. He was the youngest of their servants and probably the strongest.

But Tiggy shook her head and somehow staggered to her feet. 'Felipe?'

'They took him too,' Madre managed to say between sniffles.

The brine in Tiggy's head suddenly began to leak from her eyes. Her throat tightened and her chest throbbed. She skimmed the ground quickly for her father's slumped form. He wasn't there. For a slither of a moment, she remembered what hope felt like: Padre was OK. She turned to the collection of onlookers, spun her woozy head from side to side – if Padre was OK, where was he?

'Where's Padre?' she asked, her voice so small it could have belonged to an infant.

Madre absorbed Tiggy into a bear hug. The scent of her perfume and the soft folds of her frock soothed Tiggy, if only for a moment. 'He woke up and followed them,' Madre gasped. 'He's gone to get his ship.'

Tiggy jerked from the embrace as though her mother had delivered a lightning bolt directly to her skin. 'We need to help,' she said.

Madre shook her head. 'And what are *we* going to do? We don't know how to shoot a gun or wave a sword.'

Tiggy backed away, dodging Madre's grabbing hands. 'We can at least try. Padre showed me how to swing a sword, and I must have watched him load his rifle a hundred times when we shot apples in the courtyard.'

'Antigua, this is not a game,' Madre shrieked.

But Tiggy was already bolting down the hill. Madre was right. It wasn't a game. It was a matter of life and death. And there was no way she was going to sit at home like a good little girl while those dastardly pirates ripped her family apart at the seams. As she ran, the wind caressed her cheek, carrying on it the scent of the sea and the saddest voice Tiggy had ever heard. *I'm sorry*, the voice called. *I'm so sorry. But I promise you, somehow I will make this right.*

Despite the sorrow muting its tone, Tiggy recognized the voice as the one which had pleaded for help earlier that evening. She paused to wiggle a finger into her ear. 'Hello,' she called out.

Nothing.

'Who's there?' Tiggy called again.

Silence. Frustrated, she shook the voice from her head and continued towards the port.

She had a job to do.

CHAPTER 10

Clara opened her eyes, her chest tight and her gills frozen as she replayed the image of the boy with the one-eyed bear torn from his home by a giant crab. What had she done?

This was all her fault. If only she hadn't ignored her sister's advice and swum so close to ships. Yet Clara had grown up alongside rumours that pirates was responsible for the disappearance of her beloved madre all those years ago, so she was always drawn to the swoosh of passing boats, no matter how improbable it was that they would lead her to her mother.

She sighed. It was as though her heart itself groaned whenever she thought of her madre's easy laugh and sweet voice, and her unthinkably long purple tail which cut through the waves like a shark fin. The weight of loss was so great, sometimes Clara feared she would break. Still, it was no excuse. She should have stayed away from the galleon, she should have been stronger and withstood the attack of the eels, and she should have risen above the pain and protected the Bloodmoon prophecy.

Finally, she gave way to the tears, allowing her gills to suck in great billowing sobs of water.

'I'm sorry,' she cried to the girl in the coral dress. 'I'm so sorry. But I promise you, somehow I will make this right.'

Clara watched as the girl in her vision slowed. 'Hello,' the girl called out.

Clara froze. The girl had heard her. Even without the help of the ocean, even without salt water filling her lungs, the girl had heard her.

'Who's there?' the girl called out.

The link between them was surely growing, strengthening.

Clara couldn't help but smile.

There was still hope.

CHAPTER 11

By the time Tiggy arrived at the port, the pirates had disappeared, and it was as if they'd stolen the soul of Haven. Gone was the laughter which drifted from the taverns, the bustle of drunken sailors on the streets, the women dancing in their pretty frocks and the constant flow of ale. The streets were empty, except for the odd parent forlornly drifting back and forth, searching for the sons they'd never find. Tiggy wiped the tears from her face and turned towards the harbour. Only one galleon remained, the rest battered into the water by the bewitched squid, their masts poking from the surface as though still clinging to life. Was she too late?

She raced down the ghost of the harbour, pushing from her mind the memory of the colourful tarpaulins of the fishing boats and men lugging cargo, and ran on to the beach, kicking up the sand as she went. She paused only when the waves lapped at her feet, the salt water making every tiny laceration scream. With her heart thrashing wildly in her chest, she looked across the grey of the ocean. She could just make out the specks of the pirate ships disappearing into the horizon. 'No,' she whispered. The wind stole her words.

And that was when she saw it, a swirl of colossal tentacles whipping up the water. Panic and hope grabbed at her heart in equal measures. Perhaps her brother and Felipe were inside the creature's beak. Perhaps she could still reach them. She yanked up her dress and waded into the ocean, her legs moving as fast as they could against the tide, her hands reaching out as if she could somehow pull the sea creature towards her. 'STOP!' she shrieked. 'STOP!'

Yet the squid moved further and further away from shore. Soon it would vanish completely, taking all hope in its monstrous tentacles. Tiggy screamed in frustration, wishing she were a selkie or a mermaid or even a fish – her stupid land-body was slowing her down. A loud explosion drew her attention. The only remaining galleon was pelting towards the squid. She could just make out the shape of a man standing proud on the bow.

She would recognize that straight back anywhere. 'Padre?' she whispered.

The squid retreated into the depths, but the galleon did not stop, turning so its side faced the creature, the bulk of the cannons now ready to fire. Tiggy expected the creature to dive deep into the ocean, for surely the sight of those cannon-mouths, glinting in a line, would be enough to strike terror into anyone's heart, squid included. But the creature seemed to rise even higher from the waves, as though squaring up to its opponent in a fighting ring.

The rumbling of the cannons began, hurling a constant string of missiles in the sea creature's direction, unleashing a storm across the sea. Was Padre really going to sink the squid? He must know that Diego and Felipe were on the pirate ships – he would never fire so freely upon his own son. Optimism grew in Tiggy's heart. Perhaps if he killed the squid, or more specifically the mage inside the squid, the magic would be broken, then there would be a chance the armies of the other Fortune Isles could rescue the boys.

But the flame of hope was extinguished as if a wave had permeated her chest, and Tiggy watched in horror as the mighty squid rose from the water, tentacles whirling like dark streamers in the distance. Padre leant forwards at the bow. A fresh surge of cannonballs fired. The squid opened its chasm of a beak, releasing a burst of turquoise light, and something both dreadful and truly magical occurred before Tiggy's tear-soaked eyes: the cannonballs slowed mid-air and began to erode, as though dissolving in the wind.

'Sweet Kraken,' she whispered.

No more than wisps of smoke, the cannons drifted into the sea, paving the way for the monstrous squid. It leapt forwards, tentacles drawn beneath its body, and pounced towards the galleon swiftly, ferociously, more like a panther than a flailing sea beast.

'NO!' Tiggy roared into the waves.

She heard the thwack of wood as the squid slammed into the side of the ship. She froze, statue-still and terrified. A huge tremor travelled from the ocean floor up her legs and she watched as the tallest wave she'd ever seen swelled towards her. She managed to gasp a quick mouthful of air before the ledge of salt water knocked into her, filling her nostrils, her eyes, and threatening to drag her under. She dug in her feet and leant forwards, refusing to give in to the pressure.

Her vision cleared and she watched the squid as it seemed to sit back and admire its handiwork. Then, with an almighty roar, it dunked beneath the waves, the blue light fading into the gloom of the ocean. Her eyes moved back to the wounded galleon. A great chunk of the hull was missing and scraps of wood and bits of sails now bobbed around it like confetti. Already, the mighty ship laboured, tilting on its side. Tiggy heard a deafening creak, the crash of water and the screams of men, and suddenly the ocean gulped down the stern.

'Padre,' she cried. Panic shook her limbs into action and she launched herself at the waves. Salt water filled her mouth and her ears, her soaking ballgown felt like a thousand hands dragging her to the bottom of the sea, but she didn't stop swimming, her arms slicing into every wave like a knife. She reached the smaller pieces of broken wood, the bits which had flown the furthest from the ship, and paused to scan the wreckage for Padre. The waves ripped into her face and she could see only black and spray. 'Padre,' she cried again.

Nobody replied.

The galleon was now a drowning beast which struggled to keep its head above water. Only the bow remained clear of the ocean and even that was descending with speed. Ships didn't sink *that* fast. Injustice filled Tiggy's chest – the squid was laced with a wicked sorcery. Padre hadn't stood a chance. She watched with tears in her eyes as the galleon gasped its final breath and a great gurgle of waves swallowed it up for ever.

'No,' she whispered. She swam a few more strokes before butting up against a piece of floating ship. Only as she grabbed hold of its wooden sides did she realize her body was about to give way, wracked with exhaustion and loss. She scrambled on to her make-shift raft and, shivering from cold and desperation, searched the darkness for her father's face, listening through the thrum of her heart for his cry.

But he was gone.

'Padre!' she screamed. 'Padre, please.'

But only the roar of the ocean replied.

Tiggy wasn't sure how long she lay on her raft, gazing at the star-dappled sky and trembling beneath the drenched cloth of her dress. Perhaps it was minutes, perhaps it was hours. Time had lost all meaning. She turned her aching head and realized that she could no longer see the beach. And even though she knew this was bad, even though she knew she had no fresh water and no compass, she simply didn't care.

First Diego, then Felipe. And finally Padre.

She had lost everything.

Sailors said that every man, woman and child who died at sea ended up in a special place, locked at the bottom of the ocean for eternity. They called it Davy Jones's locker. And perhaps that wouldn't be such a bad fate for her – at least she would be with Padre.

Something surfaced from the water beside her. Tiggy flinched and raised her arms as if to defend herself, Madre's warnings of sea creatures resounding in her head. Its whiskers twitched and its black eyes shone. It was a harmless seal, clearly no threat. She lowered her arms, only to notice a silver winkle shell hanging from the creature's neck.

'Have you come to help me?' Her words ran together.

The seal responded by nudging the raft with its nose. Tiggy felt the wood move with purpose beneath her. Disorientated, cold and dense with fatigue, she let her eyes flicker shut whilst the gentle thump of the seal's nose against the raft reminded her of ticking watches, the click of beetles at night and her good friend Felipe. She watched with curiosity as the moon faded into black.

CHAPTER 12

Clara watched the dreadful scene unfold in her mind's eye, weeping as the girl's brave padre sank beneath the waves. At least the girl now lay upon a makeshift raft, being shunted to shore by a selkie in seal form. The guilt threatened to swallow Clara whole. She *had* to make this right, she had to reach out to the girl and somehow help her find her little brother.

And she had to do it before the Bloodmoon appeared in two days.

Clara scowled. Their link had strengthened, but

to communicate more than a few words would surely be impossible. Still, the girl was soaked in the salt water, and was fast asleep, probably dreaming, which would perhaps make her mind more penetrable, the barriers of consciousness naturally lowered. So with the heat of determination deep in her heart, the mermaid closed her eyes and let her story unfold . . .

Tiggy knew immediately that she was dreaming because she was swimming deep beneath the surface of the ocean, and instead of legs she had a fishtail, stretching beneath her with a long violet tailfin, which eventually turned into a single curved point, and was dotted with scales which shone rainbow-like, as though holding pockets of the sun. Tiggy had never seen a mermaid up close before, and was fascinated by how her tail looked less like the symmetrical tail of a fish and more like a giant fish-hook. She gave it a mighty flick and shot forwards in a cloud of bubbles. A squeal of delight caught in her throat. She inhaled water through the sides of her ribs and touched beneath her armpits to feel the slits which formed her gills. Laughing and breathing in the water, she pirouetted between the fish.

Just then, she noticed something overhead. The dark shadow of a gigantic ship blocking out the sun. She heard a woman's voice sounding in her head. *Stay away from the ships, Clara. Gone is the time when man welcomed sea creatures.* Tiggy wondered who the voice belonged to and who Clara might be, but the ship was looming closer and closer and curiosity nipped at Tiggy's fins. Besides, it was only a dream, so what harm could one little peek do?

She was barely at the surface when the ropy fingers of a fishing net cut through her skin. She flipped and writhed but to no avail, and the net hauled her from the water into the heat of the air. She landed with a slap against the wood of the hull, and before she could even scream, rough hands grabbed her and carried her deep into the bowels of the galleon.

And there, in the corner of a wooden chamber, heaped with treasures and strange, dead creatures with glassy eyes, was a tank, filled to the brim with water and seaweed. Tiggy opened her mouth to scream, but the dream seemed to dissolve, colours swirling like ink in water, and the next thing Tiggy knew, she was inside the tank looking straight into the eyes of a tall, well-dressed pirate. Tiggy recognized the light which crackled between his hands, the impossibly cruel slant to his face. It was the mage from the squid. Movement from above caught her eye, and when she looked up she saw a network of eels.

Her voice emerged strong. 'You have forgotten that they will not harm me, pirate.'

Tiggy couldn't believe it. That voice . . . it was the same as the voice which had reached across the sea. The voice which had called for help, the voice which had apologized and promised to make things right. Tiggy tried to think through the mist of the dream, tried to make sense of what was happening, but the sun was in her eyes and she had this inescapable sense that she was being lifted, out of the tank and away from the land of sleep.

Tiggy blinked. It was morning. She was warm and safe and tucked up in bed, though instinct told her immediately it wasn't hers. She sat up, head reeling, and looked around. Marina and Felipe's room came into focus – she was in the Signum tavern in Felipe's bed, and just across from her, Marina slept soundly.

Her mind returned to the dream. It was so real, as though she were a mermaid herself. Was the magical creature reaching out to her? She'd heard that merfolk were psychic, that they could sometimes link with each other across the sea, but she had never heard of a mermaid linking to a human. Yet last night had further blurred the line between reality and fantasy. If a man could ride inside a giant squid, then why couldn't she link with a mermaid? And if that particular mermaid was captured by the mage from the giant squid, then perhaps she knew where Diego and Felipe were.

Hope fluttered in her chest.

She sat up in bed and her memory of the night before spooled inside her head, starting with the arrival of the enchanted squid and ending with the seal pushing her to shore. Of course, that was why she was back at the tavern; after transforming back into a woman, Gabriella had carried her back to the only safe place she knew.

A sense of wonderment and panic stirred inside. Yesterday, magic had belonged solely in the ocean, to mermaids and selkies. It barely touched her world, other than through legends and stories, through dressing-up costumes and Bloodmoon celebrations. Now it was banging down her front door with heavy, inescapable fists.

Voices drifted up the stairs, pulling her from her thoughts. One belonged to Gabriella and the other sounded familiar, reassuring . . . could it be her own madre? Throwing back the covers, Tiggy saw that she was wearing one of Marina's floral-patterned nightshirts. Carefully, she crept across the floor to Marina's bed, worried that the slightest creak might bring her mother flying into the room. Her legs ached and her joints seemed to judder, but she made it to her friend without disturbing even the house mites. 'Marina,' she whispered.

Marina opened a bleary eye. 'Tiggy? You're awake.' She sat up, rubbing her head. Guilt surfaced on her sleepy face. 'I'm so sorry I didn't help you last night. If I'd have followed you like Felipe did, then maybe . . . maybe . . .'

Tiggy squeezed her friend's hand. 'Hush, there was nothing you could have done.'

'But I could have tried. I was just so scared.' Her words faded, tears gathering in her eyes. She took a moment to compose herself. 'Are you OK? Madre said she found you on the beach, half drowned.'

Tiggy shook her head. 'I think your madre found me on a raft, lost at sea.'

Marina gasped. 'Was she . . . ?'

Tiggy nodded. 'Yes. She was a seal.'

Marina blinked rapidly, as though processing the information tickled her eyes. 'I always knew she was a selkie.'

'I think everyone knows. Did you see how they flocked to the tavern last night? They needed her protection.'

'But that doesn't mean I'm a . . .' Marina tailed off, studying her hands as though they might transform into flippers right before her eyes.

'Not necessarily. Though they say that most girls born of a selkie have the gift too.'

Marina frowned. 'It's hardly a gift, Tiggy. I can't see Salvador wanting to dance with a seal.'

'Is my madre here?' Tiggy asked. Salvador was the last thing on her mind.

'Yes, she turned up soon after we put you to bed. She was beside herself. She thought she'd lost all three of you.'

Shame pricked at Tiggy's cheeks like heated pins. She wiped it away with fierce hands.

'In the name of Kraken,' Marina whispered, 'why steal our boys?'

'The curse.' Tiggy said the word as though the

syllables themselves could bite. 'Perhaps the mage has reawakened the curse.'

'But the curse of Haven, the Pirate King, Sea Golems . . . surely they're just stories.' Marina picked up Tiggy's mask, which lay strewn on the bedside table, the papier mâché still heavy with sea water. 'It can't be real.'

The memory of Diego snuggled in bed, listening intently to the tale of the Sea Golems, caused Tiggy's eyes to smart. She swallowed. Her mouth still tasted of the sea. 'What if they're more than that? I mean, yesterday a mage turned up in a giant squid and your madre turned into a seal. Why not Sea Golems? I mean, what do we actually know about ocean witchcraft?'

'I know, I know, it's just . . . it's too awful to think about.' Marina paused. 'So do you think the curse has awakened?'

'I hope not,' Tiggy replied. 'That would mean only one thing for our brothers.'

Marina's eyes grew glassy, and Tiggy instinctively rested a comforting hand on her friend's arm. Marina shook her head. 'But even if the Pirate King *was* real, he was killed centuries ago. So who was the mage from last night?'

'It's a mystery,' Tiggy said. 'There have been other sorcerers, pirates who have grown so close to the ocean they've learnt to harness her magic. But I've only ever heard of them using hexes for healing or steering boats – never have I heard of anyone, man or magical sea creature, perverting the ocean's magic into something so bad. Not since the Pirate King.'

'Perhaps another sea sorcerer has become as powerful,' Marina said. 'Maybe he's related to the Pirate King in some way. These powers might get passed in bloodlines, a bit like selkie powers.'

The girls stared at each other.

'So what do we do now?' Marina asked. 'Wait for the armies to arrive from the other islands of the Fortune Isles. Hope they track down the pirates and find our brothers?'

Tiggy punched her fist into the quilt, determination hardening her resolve. 'No. There isn't time. If the curse has awakened, then our brothers could be transforming as we speak. We must find them ourselves.'

'What?'

'We find a boat and we set sail today.'

Marina gaped at her, sucking on words which never quite left her mouth.

Tiggy frowned. 'Marina? Did you hear me?'

'But . . . but how?' Marina finally stuttered. 'All the boats have been destroyed, and nobody knows where the boys are.'

Tiggy smiled, absent-mindedly touching the sides of her chest, the place where her gills had rested in her dream. 'That's not true. There is *somebody* out there who knows.'

Marina shook her head, confused.

'She's been trying to communicate with me,' Tiggy said.

'Who?' Marina lifted a hand to Tiggy's forehead, checking her temperature. 'Are you sure you're OK? You've been through so much.'

Tiggy knocked Marina's hand away. 'There's a mermaid, held captive by the same mage who arrived in the squid and, I don't know how, but she's been calling to me, reaching out to me across the sea. If anyone knows how to find our brothers, it's her.'

CHAPTER 13

After dressing quickly, Tiggy and Marina snuck from the tavern through the basement and out the back door. The bright spark of morning hit Tiggy's eyes, and for a moment it was almost impossible for her to imagine that the terrors of last night were anything more than a nightmare. Carefully, she picked her way over the bags of rubbish and empty kegs, relieved to be wearing Felipe's spare dungarees and a pair of Marina's boots as opposed to the peach monstrosity she'd left heaped on the bedroom floor. She took Marina's hand and the pair ducked low, heading down the back alley and skimming beneath the open window of the kitchen. Madre's voice drifted towards her: 'Maybe I should just tell her the truth, Gabriella. Maybe she's old enough to know.'

Every bone in Tiggy's body seemed to harden so that she came to a standstill beside the whispering window. Was Madre talking about her?

Tiggy leant in closer, but before she could learn any more, Marina tripped on her petticoats and scuffed her knee against the wall, causing her to squeak with pain.

'What was that?' Gabriella asked. The sound of a chair scraping against the kitchen tiles sent Tiggy's heart into overdrive and, without exchanging a glance, Tiggy and Marina scuttled down the alley, away from Gabriella's prying eyes and Madre's mysterious secret.

They reached the street and finally allowed their backs to straighten.

'What do you think Madre was talking about?' Tiggy asked.

Marina shrugged and tucked a strand of dark hair behind her ear. 'At least my madre isn't the only mother keeping secrets.' She paused. 'Sorry I'm so clumsy at the moment. It's like my body and my brain have fallen out or something.'

Tiggy linked arms with her best friend. It was so good to feel close to her again. 'Well, I'll keep hold of you so you don't injure yourself.'

'Thanks,' Marina replied, leaning into Tiggy's arm. They hurried down the street, weaving between the debris of last night's raid – broken glass, smashed-up doors, shattered vases which had been used as makeshift weapons. A tremor of grief passed through Tiggy's heart as she stepped over the skeleton of a broken crib. Tonight was the second day of the Bloodmoon celebrations – the town should be filled with children wearing sea costumes and stuffing their pockets with treats, but she suspected the streets would stay empty tonight.

A few dazed rock crabs zigzagged around the wreckage, looking as though they'd consumed too much grog. Had they been affected by the mage's sorcery too? On any other occasion, she would have scooped them up and returned them to the sea, avoiding their nippers and stroking their peach-mottled shells, but today, there was no time. She had to focus on Diego and Felipe.

They stepped over a broken cot. 'Oh, Tiggy,'

Marina said, her eyes lingering on the jagged frame. 'Do you think they're OK?'

Tiggy nodded, so firmly her teeth chattered in her jaw. 'Of course they are.' She hated how her words trembled.

'How do you know this mermaid isn't just, you know . . .'

'A figment of my imagination?' Tiggy finished for her.

Marina nodded.

'I don't,' Tiggy replied. 'But it's all we've got, isn't it?'

'Well, my madre basically showed us her sealskin last night. Who am I, daughter of a selkie, to question your mermaid visions?' She grinned.

And even though it was the quickest of flashes, it was still the first time Tiggy had seen her friend smile in ages, and it immediately warmed her aching heart. 'Thanks, Mari,' she whispered.

They reached the port and their grip on each other instantly tightened, their breath snagging in their lungs. What they'd seen in the streets was nothing compared to the carnage which stretched before their feet; the port was barely recognizable.

Tiggy gulped down another wave of tears – her

beloved pier had all but vanished, leaving only the supporting posts jutting from the water so they marked the ghostly shape of what had been. The harbour was bare and lifeless, like a giant room stripped of all its furniture and soul: the colourful stalls and makeshift barrel-chairs had been reduced to rubble, a graveyard disturbed only by the movement of ripped awnings flapping in the breeze and the occasional seaman picking through the ruins, looking for something he would probably never find. And without the great curves of the square-riggers and galleons, the stone lip of the earth met the blue of the sea in a stark, angry line. Only a few smaller boats – fishing vessels and sloops – bobbed pitifully in the waves, like lost infants missing the comforting shadows of their parents.

'What have they done?' Tiggy whispered, tears finally winding down her cheeks.

Marina opened her mouth to reply, but only a whimper escaped.

Beyond the port, the beach swept away from them; dark patches of blood and the gleam of weaponry stained the golden sands, a reminder of where the dead and injured had fallen only hours ago.

A strange knocking sound pulled Tiggy's attention to the water below. The sea was bumping a collection of debris against the wall of the harbour as though trying to deliver it home – there were pieces of masts, planks, tables and chairs, stretches of cloth and the odd shoe, all tangled together and moving as one with the rhythm of the waves so that it resembled the strangest of fishing nets. Nothing was safe from the memory of the attack, not even the ocean herself.

That was when she noticed him, Diego's one-eyed bear sloshing amongst the rubble with a single paw raised, as though trying to attract her attention. 'Bobo,' she gasped, flattening her stomach against the rock so she could scoop him from the tide.

'Best not stare too long,' a voice said from behind them.

They spun to see Lucia. The ex-pirate looked tired, bedraggled, and a long cut yawned across her right cheek, yet she still managed to squeeze out a smile. 'They've done a right job, haven't they?'

Tiggy nodded, clutching the sodden bear to her chest. 'Who were they?'

Lucia dodged the question, rubbing her hand across her injured face, blood smearing towards her chin. 'Did they take your brothers?'

'Yes,' Tiggy and Marina replied together.

Lucia pulled them both into a giant hug. She smelt of sweat, copper and the sea. 'I'm so sorry,' she eventually said, releasing them and straightening her shirt. 'I tried my best to stop them, we all did, but—'

Tiggy had never heard Lucia lost for words before, and this disturbed her nearly as much as the wreckage of a port, as if the raid had damaged the people as well as the land. After a long pause, completely out of conversation, Lucia turned and walked back down the harbour.

'Where are you going?' Tiggy called after her.

'To see how the *Resolute* is shaping up. The crew's working on her now.'

Tiggy and Marina looked at each other, a flicker of hope in their eyes. Then, quick as a flash, they caught up to Lucia, circling in front of her.

'The *Resolute*? As in, your ship?' Tiggy said.

Lucia frowned. 'Yep.'

'It survived the raids?' Marina garbled.

Lucia nodded. 'It's so old and battered, the squid probably mistook it for a piece of driftwood.'

Tiggy laughed – a bird-like trill. 'Lucia, we *need* a boat. That's why we're here.'

Lucia didn't respond, her face stilled by doubt.

'I know how to reach the mage,' Tiggy continued. 'The one from the squid. We can rescue the boys.'

Lucia's face remained immobile. She stared at Tiggy long and hard, and then in one sudden motion flung back her head and roared with laughter.

'What?' Tiggy demanded, her skin hot with anger.

Lucia seemed to swallow, spluttering on her words. 'Oh, Tiggy, dear-heart, I'm sorry, I don't mean to laugh, it's just . . . how could you possibly know where the mage is? And even if you did, you are powerless against him. We all are. Didn't you see?' She leant in closer in case the waves should hear. 'He controlled the sea creatures. That kind of power hasn't existed since—'

'The Pirate King,' Tiggy said, her voice peaking with frustration.

Lucia scowled. 'Exactly. And yet you speak of rescuing the boys like it is a game.' She turned, striding down the port with purposeful steps. 'Now, go home,' she called over her shoulder. 'Before you get hurt.'

But going home was the last thing on Tiggy's

mind. For what was home without Padre and Diego? What was home without Felipe? She tucked the soggy teddy into her shirt and chased Lucia once again, catching her by the sleeve. 'Please, Lucia. I know this isn't a game. I've been hearing things . . .' She decided just to tell the truth, no matter how bizarre it sounded. 'I heard the voice of a mermaid. And I saw her too – she's been held in a tank by the same sorcerer who raided the island last night. She promised to make everything right. She'll show us how to reach the boys, I know she will.'

Tiggy expected laughter to erupt from Lucia's mouth again, but instead, the ex-pirate's face welled with pity. 'Oh, Tiggy. I have seen this happen to even the toughest of seafolk. Stress undoes our sanity. You need rest, food, before your mind falls apart completely.' She turned to leave, her black braid flipping over her shoulder.

Tiggy looked at Marina, fresh out of ideas.

'Didn't she used to be a pirate?' Marina whispered.

'And?'

'And . . . what can a pirate never say no to?'

The realization hit Tiggy like a fist. 'Wait,' she shouted after Lucia, desperation forcing her voice into a spike. 'I can pay you. I have jewellery, the odd coin – you can have it. All I ask in return is the use of your ship and your crew for a few days. And if I'm wrong, if my mind is falling apart, what harm will it do? You'll be richer, and I'll finally rest knowing I've done all that I can.'

Very slowly, Lucia turned, the dilemma playing out on her face. Lucia had a kind heart and would struggle to accept jewellery from a friend, yet she also longed for the glint of gems, for the slip of gold chains as they silked through her fingers. Once a pirate, always a pirate.

And a pirate can never say no to treasure.

CHAPTER 14

With Madre still at the tavern, Diego stolen by pirates and Padre taken by the sea, Tiggy's house was eerily silent – she could hear only the buzz of the servants as they exchanged sad words and tried to dust the house back to normality. After taking her mother's jewellery and a few gold coins stashed in one of Padre's jackets, Tiggy wrote Madre a quick note:

I've gone to find Diego and Felipe. Please try not to worry, though I know you will. I'm sorry I took

your jewellery, I had to pay for the hire of a boat.
Love, Tiggy

Marina read the words and then nodded her approval. 'Quick and to the point.'

'I didn't want to drop Lucia in it.'

'Very wise.'

They waited till Cook was in the garden and then stripped the larder, filling a sack with bread, cold meats and jars of pickles. Tiggy noticed that as long as she kept moving, as long as she forced her body to act and she didn't sit with the sadness, she felt just about human. It was as if she could escape the grief, the sight of her little brother carried away by a spider crab, the sound of the ocean swallowing her beloved Padre. So, brutal though it seemed, she kept on going, hurrying down the hill towards the port and leaving the shadow of her former life behind.

Tiggy found Lucia with ease. She was standing at the far end of the port beside the only remaining vessel. The cut on her face was beginning to crust over, and she was yet to clean off the dried blood – an angry streak reached from her cheek to her neck. A selection of workers busied themselves on board, slapping tar on to the planks and prepping the main sail. A man with dark skin and a shaved head was hanging over the side, paintbrush poised, and lovingly applying the final touches to the ship's name. The *Resolute*. Lucia watched on with a narrow smile, passing an eyeglass between her hands.

The *Resolute* had been built as a pirate ship and although it had been in the service of traders for several years, it still bore the marks of its origins. It was a sloop, smaller than Padre's square-rigger but larger than a fishing boat, and its long body and shallow hull could cut through the water with the agility of a fish, catching the larger, unsuspecting galleons in the blink of an eye. Tiggy knew that this sloop hadn't chased a galleon in years, that its decks were used for stacking piles of freshly caught fish or merchant's cloths rather than piles of treasure or injured sailors, but she could still feel the memory of adventure leaking from its wooden shell, like sap from a tree.

Marina squeezed Tiggy's hand. 'Do you think there are beds on board?'

'Hammocks,' Tiggy replied.

Marina scrunched up her nose. 'Chamber pots?'

'Buckets.'

'Soap?' Marina squeaked.

Tiggy raised an eyebrow. 'Now you're just being silly.'

Marina paused. 'Well, OK then,' she eventually said, clearly resigned to several days of discomfort.

Lucia relieved Tiggy of the jewellery and coins. 'And you're sure you want to do this?' she asked, slipping a ruby bracelet over her hand and admiring the deep, scarlet fire as it flashed against her skin. 'Traipse across the ocean on the say-so of a fictitious mermaid.'

Doubt gathered the edges of Tiggy's stomach together so that it seemed to contract into a tight knot. She hadn't heard anything from the mermaid in the tank since her dream this morning. What if she had imagined the whole thing? Her eyes were momentarily drawn across the sea . . . somewhere, Felipe and her little brother were imprisoned, possibly awaiting their transformation into Golems, if it hadn't already happened.

She inhaled deeply. 'Yes. I'm sure.'

'OK, hop on board and I'll introduce you to the crew.' Lucia helped Tiggy and Marina wobble across the gangplank until their feet landed on the solid wood of the *Resolute*'s deck. The ship seemed to groan a greeting.

The man who had been painting the name on the ship approached them. He grinned, revealing a gold tooth which glinted in the mid-morning sun; it matched the gold hoop in his ear, and Tiggy almost giggled at the thought of him selecting complementary jewellery each morning. 'A couple of landlubbers,' he said, holding out a hand and dripping paint on the deck. 'I'm Miguel, the ship's boatswain.'

'Boatswain?' Tiggy asked.

'Yeah, I look after the sloop, make sure she's sea-ready. I've been fixing a hole in the stern all morning.'

'More like all year,' Lucia muttered.

Marina arched her brows. 'A hole? That doesn't sound good.'

'You're welcome to choose another ship.' Miguel gestured to the rubble bobbing all around them.

Marina shook her head.

'Quite right,' he said, patting the side of the *Resolute* as though she were a thoroughbred horse. 'She's still more boat than hole, and that's more than can be said for the rest of those fancy Navy galleons.' He cackled.

Another man approached them. He had long, black locs held in place by a red bandanna, and skin which had been in the sun too long – red and slightly crispy. A darning needle was poised between his dirty fingers.

Lucia frowned and gestured to the needle. 'That better not be coming anywhere near my face.'

The man nodded firmly, wiping the needle on a piece of bloodied cloth. 'That cut won't hold together on its own, Captain. It'll get infected and then you've got two options: we can throw you overboard for smelling like rotten fish eggs, or you can die on board from the fever. Your choice.'

Lucia offered a reluctant shrug. 'OK, you win. Miguel, can you finish the introductions?'

Miguel nodded as the man with locs led a very reluctant Lucia into the crew's quarters below.

'That was Doc,' Miguel said, gesturing to the needle-wielding man. 'The ship's resident doctor.'

'He's a real doctor?' Marina asked, unable to keep the disbelief from her voice.

Miguel shrugged. 'Dunno, we've never asked.'

Tiggy suddenly felt a little afraid, standing on the deck of the *Resolute* with a group of ex-pirates. *They're just people*, she told herself, forcing her lungs to slow.

'Doc should wear a hat,' Marina said, trying to be helpful. 'The sun's playing havoc with his skin.'

Miguel chuckled. 'That be grog blossom, Señorita Marina.' Noticing her blank stare, he added, 'The Doc's rather partial to a glass or five of rum.'

'Oh,' Marina replied, clearly a little worried about leaving Lucia in his care.

'I'll introduce you to Cannon,' Miguel said.

'Cannon?' Tiggy asked.

'Yeah. She's responsible for all the weapons on board, cannons included.' He made a cone around his mouth with his hands and bellowed towards the front of the ship, 'Oi, Cannon!'

Tiggy awaited her arrival, imagining a woman with broad shoulders and large hands, someone who could juggle cannonballs before breakfast. When Cannon didn't appear, Miguel caught Tiggy's eye and winked. 'This ought to do the trick,' he whispered, before shouting, 'Grub's up.'

A small woman with short brown hair and scrawny arms seemed to appear from nowhere. She had this startled look, like she was about to start firing or had just stopped. 'Did somebody say something about food?' She spoke loudly, as though her hearing was damaged, and played nervously with the leather strap which was slung diagonally across her shirt, boasting an array of bullets and tools.

Miguel shook his head. 'You need to clean out them ears, must be full of gunpowder or summit. We've got guests.'

Cannon forced a smile, though it looked like it pained her. 'Hi, I'm Cannon. Because, well, you know, I man the cannons.' A look of sadness pulled at her pointed face, softening it for a moment. 'At least, I used to.'

'You never know,' Miguel said. 'One day we'll get attacked and we'll really need you.'

'Chance would be a fine thing.' She looked directly at Tiggy. 'Since Captain decided we should go straight, you know, honest, nobody bothers with us any more. Except for last night, of course . . . and where was I? Fast asleep on the floor of a leaky old tavern.' Her voice wavered with emotion.

Tiggy didn't know what to say. The way Cannon was talking, it was as though her favourite pet had died, not that bloodshed was hard to come by. Tiggy paused, before saying, 'Sorry,' though it sounded more like a question than a genuine response.

Cannon smiled regardless, clearly pleased with any sympathy she could get. 'Captain tells us we're taking you on a voyage.' Her eyes darted to the sack at Tiggy's feet. 'What's in there?'

'Just some supplies.' She slid the sack towards Cannon with her foot.

Cannon's eyes lit up. 'I *knew* someone mentioned food.' She grabbed the bag with hungry fingers and darted into the crew's quarters below.

'That's for all of us, you greedy sea cucumber,' Miguel yelled after her. He turned to Tiggy and Marina. 'Anyway, come on, take a look at the crew's quarters and grab yourself a hammock.' He gestured to the stairs which led to the front belly of the sloop. 'We're about to set sail.'

Just then, a boy leapt from the crow's-nest and climbed down the netting which extended from the mast. His legs seemed to move faster than his arms, causing his foot to catch in some rigging. He tumbled head first towards the decking, but the rope thankfully tightened just in time so that he dangled before them, upside down and rotating slowly. 'Hi,' he said, completely unfazed, as though hanging like a big-eared bat were a normal everyday occurrence. 'I'm Spider.' He looked about the same age as Tiggy and Marina, with light brown skin and a shock of black hair.

'Worst spider I've ever seen,' Miguel muttered. 'More like a drunken barrel-mite.'

'I'm the navigator,' Spider said, a grin zipping across his face. 'You'd be lost without me. Ha! Get it? Lost without me, cos I'm a navigator.'

Miguel paused to roll his eyes. 'Lad thinks he's a comedian.'

'So where are we taking you?' Spider asked. 'It kinda helps if I know where I'm aiming.'

'I . . . I don't know yet.' Tiggy wondered why she was the one faltering on her words when she wasn't the one spinning from a rope. 'Maybe just sail free of the other Fortune Isles, then it'll come to me.' She needed to hear the mermaid again, but she just didn't know how.

Spider studied her face for a moment. 'You're a canvas shy of a full sail, aren't you?'

Tiggy gawped at him. 'That's a bit rich.'

'So what's your nickname?' Marina asked Miguel, clearly trying to prevent a row. Tiggy smiled gratefully at her.

Miguel straightened up, twiddling the ring in his ear for a moment. 'Nickname?'

'You know,' Marina said. 'Cannon, Spider, Doc . . . What does everyone call you?'

'Miguel,' he said, confusion taking up lodgings on his broad face. 'I thought I told you.'

Spider whooped with laughter. 'No point cracking on with old Miguel. He's got all the humour of a sardine at lunchtime.'

'What happens to sardines at lunchtime?' Tiggy asked.

'They get eaten,' he replied, laughing.

Miguel frowned. 'Do you want down, or shall I just leave you flipping like a fish on a hook?'

Spider's laughter stopped abruptly. 'Down, please.'

'Hang on a sec.' Miguel searched his belt for a knife.

Tiggy pulled out the small dagger she'd absent-mindedly taken from the sailor the night before. 'Will this do? Just press the button and the blade pops out.'

Miguel turned the cylinder in his hand and freed the blade with a click. He released a low whistle. 'This be a fine blade, Miss Antigua.'

He was right. She felt a wave of guilt and quietly resolved to reunite it with its rightful owner once her adventure was complete.

'Don't let Cannon see,' he said, slicing the rope

from Spider's ankle. 'She'd claim it in the wink of a whale's eye.' Spider landed on the deck with a thud and Miguel chuckled, passing the blade back to Tiggy.

Lucia reappeared, pressing a cloth as firmly to her cheek as the scowl pressed into her forehead. 'Come on, you lazy barnacles, stop gossiping like a load of old washerwomen. Raise the anchor, grab yourself an oar. Let's show our passengers what this old sloop can do.'

'Aye aye, Captain,' came the collective call. The crew began busying themselves with ropes and oars, the ship suddenly bursting with life.

'Yo ho ho,' Lucia roared.

'Yo ho ho,' the crew called back.

Tiggy could hardly believe it. In just a few moments, they would be heading out to sea. She had never even been on a boat – let alone sailed beyond the Fortune Isles – never seen the arc of the horizon blurring into nothingness. Excitement caused her skin to prick all over.

'WAIT!' a voice cried, ringing across the harbour like the screech of a gull.

Tiggy turned, her heart in her mouth, expecting to see her own madre pelting towards them, skirts hitched up and legs pumping. But it was Gabriella.

'Madre,' Marina gasped.

'Quick,' Doc shouted. 'There's no time to lose.'

But Lucia raised her hands, causing the crew to pause and the *Resolute* to hover at the port a moment longer. 'We can't outsail Gabriella,' she said simply. 'Nor would we want to. Her kind have the magic of the ocean in their veins.'

Gabriella reached the *Resolute* and crossed the boarding plank with confident, graceful steps, not caring if she toppled into the waters below. She hopped on to the deck and stood over her daughter with an arched eyebrow. 'And where exactly do you think you're sneaking off to?'

'To find Felipe and Diego,' Marina replied; her voice sounded strong, even though her bottom lip quivered at the sight of her madre. It was easier to leave without looking into the eyes of your loved ones, Tiggy decided.

Gabriella placed her hands on her hips. 'But nobody knows where they are. You're searching for a needle in a haystack, an anchovy in an ocean. Come back to the tavern. I have my' – she paused, searching for the right word – 'sources. They'll report back to me.'

Tiggy presumed that Marina was referring to the

other selkies, the ones who chose to live out at sea, permanently transformed into seals.

'What if there isn't time?' Marina whispered.

Gabriella sighed and turned from her daughter, her eyes locking on the ruby bracelet which sparkled around the ex-pirate's wrist. 'Are you preying on the tender hearts of my girls, Captain?'

Lucia covered the bracelet with her spare hand. 'I tried to tell them, but they're really quite stubborn.'

Tiggy stepped forward. 'Please, Gabriella.' She wished she sounded more self-assured. 'There's a mermaid held captive in a tank by the mage. I've heard her voice, dreamt of her, and she'll show me how to find them, I know she will. She promised to make things right.'

Spider let out a snort of disbelief from the top of his mast, only to be silenced by a thunderous glare from Miguel.

Gabriella paused, her black hair twisting around her face in the sea breeze. 'A mermaid, you say?'

Tiggy nodded.

Gabriella didn't reply, but Tiggy noticed a sense of resignation settle on her features. Then she pulled a winkle necklace from her pocket, just like the one which hung from her throat, and pressed it into

Marina's open palm. 'This will protect you,' she finally whispered. 'For you are of selkie blood, born of a wave.'

Marina paused, holding the necklace at arm's length as if reluctant to accept the gift. Gently, Gabriella closed her daughter's fingers around the charm. 'One day you will be grateful for this, Mari.' She then looked at Tiggy. 'And you, Antigua de Fortune, you are still so young, yet it seems you are ready for the trials of the ocean.' She took Tiggy's hand in her own and Tiggy felt a strange tingle in the tips of her fingers, almost like a static shock.

'What trials?' Tiggy asked.

Gabriella lowered her voice. 'Your vision of a mermaid could be more dire than you think.'

Tiggy offered a stubborn shake of the head. 'She wants to help me.'

'I'm afraid her intention is not the issue.'

'What do you mean?' Tiggy asked.

'There exists a prophecy – the Bloodmoon prophecy – which speaks of the reawakening of the curse of Haven.'

The bottom fell out of Tiggy's stomach. It was as she'd feared. 'The mage will be able to turn our boys into Sea Golems?'

Gabriella nodded. 'The prophecy has always been guarded by the merfolk. They are the only ones who know the exact wording.'

'That's why he has the mermaid?' Tiggy gasped. 'And you think she's told him? Is that why she was apologizing?'

'Perhaps.' Gabriella leant into her, as if about to share a wonderful secret, but instead simply whispered, 'Find our boys and bring them home. You have until the Bloodmoon appears tomorrow night, for after that I fear they will no longer be boys.'

CHAPTER 15

All morning, Clara had desperately tried to find the girl again, yet the visions continued to evade her. She was so weak, and no matter how hard she grasped, the threads of magic kept slipping through her hands. All she'd eaten in days were scrapings of algae from the panes of her tank and the tiny sea creatures milling around in the silt below. It wasn't enough to sustain a mollusc, let alone a mermaid. And when combined with the mage's torture – the razor sting of the eels – she was beginning to feel like she was disappearing. Like she was no more substantial than the reflection before her. A half-ghost. Even the vivid purple hue of her tail was starting to fade.

She pressed her fingers together, searching for the faintest crackle of turquoise light. But there was nothing. Anger and injustice lurched inside – she would never reach the girl now. She glanced at the stuffed creatures beyond her tank. Birds, tigers, possums, some she didn't even recognize. If she didn't escape soon, perhaps she would be next.

The sound of the mage's footsteps jerked her from her thoughts. Even through the gunk of the tank, she could see his evil face was alight with mischief. 'It's time for you to go, fishface,' he said, tapping his fingernails against the glass vial which hung from his neck.

'You're releasing me?' Clara was unable to mask the joy in her voice.

The mage began to laugh. 'Good grief, no.' He paused, seeming to enjoy the devastation as it swamped her face. 'I'm simply moving your tank. And when I say *I'm moving your tank*, what I mean is, *they* are.'

He clicked his fingers and a group of pirates rushed through the door. With savage hands, they shifted her tank on to a low wooden trailer and wheeled her from the cabin, away from the glassy stare of the dead animals. The water slopped up the sides of her tank, sending the eels spiralling this way and that. It was like being caught in a whirlpool with no way out.

They reached a flight of rickety stairs and the men paused to heave her tank upwards by hand, stair by stair; each clunk reverberated through her, causing her scales to stand on end and her stomach to heave. Yet a glimpse of hope was beginning to stir inside her – perhaps they were moving her on to the deck, at least then she would feel the sun against her skin. An idea struck: if she was on the deck, she could surely send a message to the girl. *She* couldn't leap from the uncovered top of the tank – her body wasn't agile enough, for mermaids were swimmers, not leapers – but an enchanted eel could. Suddenly she was relieved that the silt eddied around her; it meant the pirates couldn't see the smile spreading across her face.

Finally, she emerged on to the deck of the great pirate galleon, but there was no sunshine, and the air which permeated her water smelt damp, thick and mossy. The vessel had docked inside a monstrous cave. She blinked back tears. For what was a cave if not an even bigger tank? She was now inside two prisons.

Think, Clara, think. The galleon must have sailed into the cave, which meant there must be a direct link to the ocean. An underground river. Excitement swelled in her stomach.

All was not lost.

The cavern was huge, big enough to house the galleon and a selection of sloops and riggers. The walls were the colour of sealskin, which meant the rock was volcanic, and glinting from every outcrop, hanging from every cluster of stones, were stacks of treasure. Jewellery, coins, multi-coloured pools of gems. The sight was dazzling, yet it still somehow paled in comparison to Clara's family reef. Her heart welled with loss.

Clara looked around her. 'You live here? Inside a dormant volcano?'

'Of course not. The cave is simply where we hide the fleet and any excess loot. Home is up there.' The mage pointed to the domed roof of the cave. 'Now, come. I have a job for you.'

The pirates wheeled her to the edge of the ship and over a small, makeshift bridge: several sturdy boarding planks led from the vessel to a peninsula of angry rock. They made a gangplank big enough to take the weight of her tank. She pressed her face to the glass. Directly below was a glistening shallow pool, which must surely stretch towards the mouth of the cave and the infinite ocean beyond. This was her one chance to send a message to the girl, so she could rescue her little brother, rescue all the boys before they were turned into Sea Golems.

Her hand shot up and grabbed an unsuspecting eel. It flipped and turned in her hand, but she held it tight and, speaking in the ancient dialect of the sea, delivered a hex straight into its slippery skin.

'*Starting as a whisper, ending with a roar,*
Carry please this message across the ocean fl'or,
Bid the fish, the dolphins too, the jellyfish and
*   whale,*
Bring to me the girl, so freedom may prevail.'

She reached deep inside her soul, and somewhere, somehow, found a fragment of remaining strength. Nobody noticed as a spark of turquoise flashed through her fingers and the tiniest drop of inky blue leached through the surrounding water. She released the eel just before the tank reached the peninsula, and watched with joy as a great slosh of water carried the eel out of the top of the tank and down, down, down, to the shallows below.

CHAPTER 16

Tiggy watched the waves fold back around them, the movement of the sloop rolling through her like a lullaby. The Fortune Isles had eventually faded into tiny specks, before vanishing completely from view, and the sea had transformed into an endless cloth of sapphire which surrounded them on all sides.

She should be in her element, yet she felt on edge, frustrated. For the past hour or so, they'd been sailing in a lazy circle, just treading water until she shared a destination, or at the very least, a direction.

But no matter how hard she listened, she couldn't hear the voice of the mermaid calling her through the blue. Perhaps if she slept, she would dream of that long, glowing tail again, but Tiggy was too filled with adrenalin to even consider taking a nap.

Diego and Felipe could be *anywhere*. Had she stolen Madre's jewellery, run away to sea, only to draw hoops in the water until supplies ran out? Tears of anger scraped at her eyes. She leant over the bow as far as she dared without falling overboard, and stared into the water below. 'Where are you?' she whispered. A solitary tear tumbled from her eye into the ocean. Tiggy could have sworn that when the tear hit the water below, it transformed into a drop of indigo paint, ink perhaps. But it happened too fast to be sure, and before she could check, the spray and the sloop had engulfed the drop entirely. She must have imagined it, desperation and loss unravelling her mind.

Marina stood beside her. 'Still nothing?' she asked, laying a gentle hand on Tiggy's arm.

Tiggy shook her head and squeezed Bobo, who still nestled safely beneath her shirt.

'If you lose something, you should retrace your steps,' Marina said softly.

Tiggy looked at her friend. 'Pardon?'

'That's the old saying, isn't it? *If something dear you have misplaced, your footsteps you must now retrace.* Maybe you should tell me about the times you heard the mermaid. Maybe there's a clue as to how we can find her again.'

Tiggy scrunched up her face, convinced it was pointless, but when she saw the eagerness in Marina's eyes, she decided to play along. 'OK, so the first time I heard her was after the Golem Ball . . .' A shadow of something passed across Marina's face. Envy? Guilt? Tiggy wasn't sure, so she pushed on regardless. 'I was dancing with Salvador and fell into the string quartet.'

Marina started to giggle, then clamped a hand over her mouth. 'Sorry.'

Tiggy laughed, and a fragment of the weight lifted from her shoulders so she could enjoy the salt on her lips and the wind in her hair. 'No, it is kind of funny looking back. I mean, not at the time. Then, I wanted the ground to swallow me up. But when Salvador went all puffy and stuck-up, it was pretty funny.'

Marina sighed. 'But to dance with Salvador. The Governor's son.'

Tiggy pushed her friend's arm playfully. 'Mari, he was a sweaty pig. And I swear he'd half-murdered some poor rodent and stuck it on his upper lip. His moustache just wouldn't stop twitching.'

'Ew.' She looked thoughtful for a moment. 'Tig, do you think Salvador has been taken too?'

Tiggy shrugged. The safety of the Governor's son was the last thing on her mind. 'Maybe. I don't think anywhere was safe from last night's raid.'

Marina sighed. 'Imagine if we rescue Salvador too...'

'Anyway.' Tiggy ignored the dreamy look in her friend's eyes. 'Just after that, Madre and I had this argument, then I ran down to the beach and fell head first into a rock pool.'

'Ouch. It really wasn't a good night.'

'It really wasn't. Anyway, it was then that I heard her for the first time. My head was submerged in salt water and ... you're going to think this is weird ... but I just lay there, feeling like I *belonged*.'

'What did she say?' Marina asked, her eyes widening.

'She asked for help.' Tiggy bit her lip in thought. 'Of course, I didn't know she was a mermaid at that point.'

Marina seemed to count the clouds for a moment, deep in her own thoughts. 'Maybe it was the salt water. Maybe it helped her reach out to you.'

'Maybe. But the next time I heard her, the pirates had taken the boys and I was on dry land, no salt water in sight.'

'Oh,' Marina said, a little deflated. 'And the dream?'

'I was at sea, floating on a piece of driftwood. I dreamt that I *was* the mermaid. With a long, violet tail which flicked at the end like a fishhook. I was captured by the pirates and stuck in a tank. And that's when I saw the mage from the squid – I'd have recognized him anywhere.'

Marina watched as a gull orbited the sails, her eyelids flickering against the sunshine. 'I still think the salt water's our best shot.'

'I could take a swim.'

A loud voice cut through the breeze. 'You will do no such thing.'

They whipped around to see Cannon. She stood behind them sharpening a short blade on a leather strap. Her brown, cropped hair ruffled in the wind and her elfin features tightened. 'Do you realize how many sea creatures are lurking beneath this sloop just waiting for one of us to be daft enough to jump in?' The rhythmic swoosh of metal against leather emphasized her words.

Tiggy and Marina shook their heads, unable to take their eyes from the gleam of the dagger.

'Aye,' Cannon said slowly, enjoying the drama. 'Humans aren't welcome in the sea. You should know this, living on Haven.'

Miguel joined them. 'Aye aye.' He shoved a bucket and scrubbing brush towards Tiggy. 'Captain says she wants the deck clean.'

'But . . . but . . . we're passengers, not crew members.' Marina's voice came out high-pitched and childlike.

'It's a small crew, so we all chip in,' Miguel replied simply. 'Spider's on lookout, Doc's at the helm, Cannon's cleaning her knife and Captain's . . . well, she's the captain, she can do as she pleases.'

'What about you?' Marina asked.

'I'm . . . I'm . . .' He dithered for a moment. 'I'm still fixing the stern.'

Before Marina could object, Tiggy nudged her and gestured towards the bucket. It was filled with fresh sea water, by far enough to dunk her head in.

Marina squeaked, realizing her friend's plan.

'That's perfect.'

Tiggy glanced at Cannon and Miguel. They were expecting her to grab the scrubber and start cleaning. Well, they were going to get a surprise; the thought almost made her laugh. She knelt down, took a huge gulp of air and dunked her head straight inside the bucket.

The world plunged into black, sounds muffled, and the water grabbed hold of her, filling her ears and nose, stuffing her eyes and mouth with salt. Yet she felt completely calm. Held safe in a world of tin and brine, she listened for the mermaid's voice, willing it to find her through layers of ocean and sea air. Nothing.

Strong hands grasped her shoulders and hauled her back into reality. She sat, blinking at Miguel, water streaming from her hair and sunshine burning her eyes, suddenly feeling very foolish. A cough scrabbled its way up her throat.

'What are you doing?' Miguel asked, still gripping her shoulders. 'I asked you to wash the decks, not your hair.'

'You only need to wash your hair once every two years,' Cannon chipped in. 'Anything more is a waste of water.'

Marina ignored them, her face alive with excitement. 'Did it work? Did you hear her?'

'Hear who?' Cannon said. 'Who, pray tell, communicates via bucket these days?'

Tiggy briefly considered lying, then decided to tell the truth, because they would probably think she was lying anyway. 'A mermaid.'

But Miguel didn't laugh. 'That's right. I heard you tell that selkie about it. There's a mermaid held captive in a tank.' A mysterious smile tugged at his lips so they could no longer contain the glint of his gold tooth.

Tiggy nodded, her face numb with cold.

'Ha!' The word burst from Cannon's lips like ammunition. 'You both got imaginations bigger than an orca pod.'

Miguel leant forward, his smile fading and his brow pulling together so that it threw his eyes into shadow. He dropped his voice so that it whistled with secrecy. 'My dear padre used to tell me tales about the merfolk and selkies. Apparently, merfolk are telepaths, which means they can talk to each other using only their minds, so it's possible you heard one.' He turned to Marina, his gaze lingering on the silver winkle around her neck. 'And selkies, they can calm even the most terrifying of beasts with no more than a song. The magic of the ocean runs deep, and after what I saw last night ...'

'We don't talk about that,' Cannon snapped, obviously still sore at missing out on the battle.

But Miguel pretended not to hear, a look of fear and nostalgia on his face. 'A mage controlling a giant squid, harnessing the sorcery of the waves even on land ... right now I will believe just about anything, Señorita Tiggy.'

Marina knelt beside Miguel. 'The first time Tiggy heard the mermaid, she'd fallen in a rock pool.'

Realization flashed across his face. 'So that's why you were dunking your head in the bucket. I just assumed you were weird.'

Cannon tutted. 'That's the first sensible thing you've said, Miguel.'

Miguel silenced Cannon with a raised hand. 'Let the girl speak.'

'It didn't work,' Tiggy said. 'I don't know why. First time I heard her, I fell and landed in a rock pool, but maybe dunking my head just isn't the same.'

Miguel tapped his stubbled chin for a moment. 'Good point. Maybe it needs to be a shock.' And with that, he picked up the bucket and hurled the contents into Tiggy's face.

Tiggy squealed. The force of the water caused her to sway backwards, cold and salt nipping at her face, her throat, her chest.

Cannon roared with laughter. 'You're as daft as they are, Miguel.'

Miguel ignored her. 'Anything?'

Tiggy shook her head, spitting up mouthfuls of water. She could hear only the swish of the sails, the drum of the waves against the hull and the laughter rolling from Cannon's mouth. She knelt on the deck, dripping, shivering and feeling completely useless. Why couldn't she hear the mermaid? How would she ever find Diego and Felipe? She looked at Marina. 'What now?' she whispered.

Just then, a voice shouted from above. 'Hey, you great sea slugs!' It was Spider. He scampered down the netting, jumped the last foot and hit the deck with a loud clunk, his eyes sparkling with wonder. 'Instead of trying to drown each other, why don't you look at the sea below?'

'What?' Tiggy asked, wiping her face with the back of her hand.

Spider grinned, his face all points and mischief. 'You gotta see it to believe it. I think that mermaid of yours has a plan.'

Miguel and Cannon were already leaning over the bow, gasping like children on Christmas morning. Tiggy and Marina had to elbow their way through to see what all the fuss was about.

Spider was right; it had to be seen to be believed. Stretching in front of the *Resolute*, just below the surface of the water, was a huge shoal of silvery fish, their iridescent bodies moving as one and forming the shape of a giant V. At their head was a single black eel.

Tiggy blinked several times, but the edges of that

arrow remained crisp and sure. 'Is that an arrow?'

'It certainly is.' Miguel turned and clipped Cannon gently around the head. 'You see, the magic of the ocean runs deep.'

He turned toward the captain's quarters at the stern of the boat and hollered with all his might. 'Captain, Captain, come quick, the fish are showing us which way to sail.'

Just then, the shoal broke formation, some of them falling backwards so they encircled the sides of the sloop, hugging the wooden planks so closely they seemed to become an extension of the vessel herself. Ever so slowly, the ship began to change direction.

'What's happening?' Marina whispered to Tiggy.

Tiggy shook her head. 'It looks as though . . .'

Doc boomed from the helm, 'What's going on? The rudder's stuck, me wheel won't turn.'

Spider began to jump up and down, causing the crow's-nest to tremble. 'They're steering the ship. The fish are steering the ship.'

'It's her,' Tiggy whispered to Marina, her voice heady with joy. 'The mermaid. It must be her. She's showing us the way.'

Marina gripped her friend's arm. 'We find the mage, we find our brothers.'

Tiggy could have wept with relief. No longer would the *Resolute* sail in circles. It had direction, purpose. And she felt it too, as if her bones mirrored the planks below.

Lucia emerged from her quarters, telescope at the ready, her face twisted with concern for her crew's state of mind. 'What's that? Fish, you say?'

'It's true,' Spider shouted. 'The fish are guiding the ship.'

'Doc?' Lucia shouted behind her.

'Well, something's steering her and it isn't me,' came the reply.

The group parted so Lucia could peer into the waters below. She gasped, her braid falling forward. 'Sweet mother of a starfish, I have never seen anything like it in all my days.' She turned towards the helm, the thrill of adventure awakening her face. 'Doc,' she bellowed, 'we've got a new navigator.'

'Oi,' Spider whined from above.

Lucia ignored him. 'Release the wheel and let the . . . erm . . . fish . . . do the work.' She pushed the telescope to her right eye and adjusted the lens slightly, scouring the horizon for land. 'Can't see nothing yet.' She turned to Tiggy and her voice emerged more heavily accented than normal. 'Well,

Antigua de Fortune, you said the mermaid would lead you to the mage, to the boys. So now there's only one question remaining.'

Tiggy raised her eyebrows, barely able to contain the excitement and relief as it simmered in her belly. 'What?'

'How are we gonna split all the treasure?'

CHAPTER 18

The pirates wheeled Clara's tank up a winding path, carved from the rock by a thousand grubby feet and the passage of time. As she reached the ceiling of the cave, the light levels grew stronger and stronger, feeding her skin with strength and hope. An opening in the stone above glowed like the entrance to heaven. Hands kept pushing, her tank kept rumbling, and within minutes she was free of the cave and basking in the sunlight. She rubbed her eyes, daring to tilt her face so the warmth hit her skin. The eels felt it too, their bodies seeming to unwind around her.

The pinnacle of the volcano now sat behind her and slumbered soundly, its fiery innards resting deep inside the earth. She wished she could rouse it, like a sleeping dragon, coughing up magma and swallowing down the hateful galleon in a wave of bubbling lava. Below, a grand castle sprouted from the base of the volcano as though the mountain had somehow sprung a leak, its molten rock rearing up and crystallizing into turrets, bridges and thick, immovable walls.

The mage turned from the front of the party and shouted back to her, 'Now *this* is home.'

But Clara was no longer staring at the castle; she was staring at the sea, for it was just a mere smudge of blue in the distance. She was completely land-bound. The thought made her shudder.

Several bumps and pushes later, Clara found herself passing beneath a monstrous lattice grille, through a set of wooden doors and into the body of the castle itself. Her tank came to a standstill inside the courtyard. She was penned in on every side by towering stone walls and turrets, the bowl of blue sky above reminding her of the ocean she had lost. Fear flickered beneath her skin, a tremble which passed right down her scales into her tailfin.

Scattered about the walls of the castle were huge cages, not much smaller than her tank, filled with a flurry of beaks and talons and feathers. Seagulls. She glanced at the mage, who smiled in return. 'They're hungry, wouldn't you say?' the villain whispered. He then turned and shouted to a burly pirate who stood at the back of the courtyard. 'Bring me the boys.'

The pirate disappeared into the arch, and after a short wait a never-ending stream of boys filled the courtyard; there were at least one hundred, ranging from tiny babes to teenagers. They huddled together like a shoal of newly hatched fish, glancing anxiously at the armed pirates who flanked their every side. The older boys cradled the infants, trying helplessly to soothe them with words and hugs, whilst pleading with the pirates for milk and bread.

Sympathy pulled at Clara's chest, followed by the sharp, puncturing pain of guilt. This was all her fault: if only she hadn't told him the words of the prophecy.

One by one, the boys turned and stared at her. Clara realized that now land walkers no longer dared to swim amongst the rocks, only a few of these boys had ever seen a mermaid before. Their faces hung slack in wonder, and for the briefest of moments she forgot the crushing guilt.

A pirate busied himself behind her, grabbing a long metal pipe and sucking on the end for a second. Clara watched as it began to trickle with water. He then stuck the pipe over the top of her tank so as to refill it. She realized for the first time that the water in her tank was getting low. The water was being siphoned from somewhere . . . Another tank buried beneath their feet? Or maybe the underground river wound its way beneath her?

The mage tapped against the pane of her tank, causing her to startle. 'I need you to show me the boy,' he said.

'Which boy?' Clara asked, feigning ignorance.

'Now, now,' the mage said, blue light flashing between his palms. 'You and I both know what happens when you play dumb.' He gestured to the eels which gathered above her head like narrow, black clouds. 'The boy from the prophecy.'

Clara shook her head. 'You honestly expect me to know which boy it is?'

'Yes. And you will tell me, or I will start executing them, one by one.'

A collective whimper rose from the crowd of

boys. Clara could sense their fear; it crackled through the air like the beginnings of a storm. 'OK,' she whispered. 'But you will need to bring them closer, as I have to see their faces.'

The pirates organized the boys into a line which snaked its way before her tank. She looked at each face – took her time, pretended to consider every feature with the utmost of care, then, without any real thought, shook her head. The mage sighed: she was buying time, and he knew it.

But the sixteenth boy. He was different. Not only was he older, on the cusp of manhood, but he wore a strange look on his face. She knew in an instant; this boy had seen mermaids before. Her eyes narrowed, recognition suddenly igniting her insides. She knew this boy.

'Felipe?' she whispered.

Felipe hobbled before the tank, struggling to keep his balance. He'd had nothing to eat or drink since they'd arrived on this hateful island, and his body ached all over. But the main reason he was wobbling was because of his leg: as soon as the pirates had bundled the boys off the galleon, Felipe had casually bent over and pretended he'd had an itch, when really he'd partially unscrewed his wooden leg. He was waiting for the right moment to use it as a weapon, for it was a sturdy piece of wood and the metal lip which sat beneath his knee was made from the hardiest of irons. And finally, the right moment had arrived.

He regained his posture and focused on the mermaid in the tank. And as he peered through the murk and the fog of his own anxiety, he finally saw her. His heart flipped and he suppressed a gasp. It was Clara: one of the merfolk who'd saved his life on the treacherous night he'd lost his leg. She looked so different, crammed into a tank and hungry for space, her hues dwindling. In the ocean, she'd resembled a wisp of colour, as graceful as a seahorse and as long as a serpent, her violet tail tapering into a singular, translucent hook and her scales shining like pouches of bioluminescent algae. He noticed that the gills at the side of her chest opened and closed more quickly than he remembered, echoing the rhythm of her chest. She was as scared as him.

He blinked a greeting, afraid to acknowledge their history in the presence of the mage. Ever so slowly, she blinked her reply. He had forgotten the detail of her face, how her angular features were edged with two pointed ears. Purple scales started at her ears, then wound down her neck and her chest almost like a bikini top, before travelling down her stomach and turning into her tail. Her eyes sparkled brilliant aqua-blue and her dark hair fanned outwards like a crown of seaweed. She was beautiful and unearthly all at once.

Questions pounded in Felipe's skull like a heart full of rage. What on earth did the mage want with Clara? What did she have to do with the boys of Haven? And why were they being marched before her like lambs to the slaughter?

Since being captured, he had been unable to fathom the agenda of the mage, though it clearly had something to do with the Bloodmoon tomorrow night and the curse of Haven. The mage had also mentioned something about a prophecy. But what did that have to do with Clara?

Well, one thing was certain, she was only of use to the mage if she remained trapped in that tank. His eyes found the metal pipe which seemed to be dripping a steady flow of water into her tank. Realizing it must be sea water, for mermaids wither in the absence of salt, he followed the pipe with his eyes: it drew a rusty line from her prison to a hole in the paving slabs. His mind whirred. A source of salt water . . . a possible escape? The hole was just about big enough for a human to slip down. For a mermaid to slip down?

The mage seemed to notice the mermaid's slow response. 'Is it him?' he asked, turquoise light trembling between his palms.

Felipe's stomach flipped, his chest tightened, his eyes fixed on the tiny ball of lightning which snapped between the mage's hands.

Slowly, firmly, Clara shook her head. 'No,' she said, her watery voice rising from the tank. 'This is not the child from the prophecy.'

The mage frowned so that his heavy brows thatched his murderous eyes. 'You're sure? You've stared at him long enough.' The light between his hands flared.

Felipe swallowed, his gaze shifting to the mage's face. Time seemed to slow and fear stuck its spindly fingers down Felipe's throat. He feared he would vomit.

'I can assure you, this is not the child from the prophecy,' Clara said.

The light faded in the mage's palms, even as anger sparked in his bloodthirsty eyes. 'You will look at every boy by sundown, sea beast. Time is running out, do you understand?'

Felipe watched Clara's eyes thin, the water beginning to swirl around her so it lifted her hair from her face and caused the eels to spiral. 'No,' she mouthed, her face locked in a stubborn grimace.

Quicker than a viper strike, the mage shot out his hand and grabbed Felipe by the neck. Shocked, Felipe didn't even try to fight back as the mage shoved him into the side of Clara's tank and lifted him from the ground. Felipe tried to cough, tried to breathe, but his throat was wreathed in pain and pressure.

Clara banged on the glass behind him. 'Let him go, please.'

The mage shook his head. 'Will you watch this innocent boy die? *All* of these innocent boys die?'

And even though Felipe's lungs burnt, his vision curling at the edges, the mage's words planted a ferocious anger in his gut. Something toughened around his heart, an armour-plating forged from courage, fury and a sense of righteousness. He simply wouldn't let the evil mage slaughter these innocent boys. Even one dead boy was too many. As the colours of the courtyard smudged into black, Felipe hatched a plan. If he freed Clara, they could swim for help, then summon the armies of the other Fortune Isles.

His fingers numb and oxygen-deprived, Felipe reached down and fumbled with the top of his wooden leg. It came free with surprising ease. And before anyone noticed, before he could lose his nerve, he swung the metal lip of his leg as hard as he could into the side of the tank. The sound of splintering glass reverberated around the courtyard, and within a heartbeat the tank had exploded, sending water and eels slopping across the floor.

The mage released Felipe as they both tumbled to the floor, swept up in the wave of salt and cold. Mustering every last ounce of strength, Felipe reached towards Clara, catching her beneath the armpits and cushioning her fall. The pirates rushed forwards, the mage summoned his turquoise light... but they were too late.

Felipe kicked his leg, the mermaid flicked her mighty tail and, with the aid of the gushing water, the pair of them slipped down the hole and into the darkness below.

CHAPTER 19

It was late afternoon when Tiggy and Marina, still leaning over the bow of the ship, watched the shoal of fish disperse, their silvery bodies dissolving back into the ocean. Tiggy gasped, disappointment clutching at her heart. 'Fish, come back.' She reached into the spray, imagining she could somehow grab those slippery bodies and pull them back, but her hands fell empty through the air and she was reminded of Padre, how quickly he had slipped from her hands. The knife of loss punctured the flesh between her ribs, robbing her of any breath.

'Are you OK?' Marina asked.

'Yeah, I just . . . I just . . . wish Padre were here.'

Marina hooked an arm around her friend's neck. 'I know, me too.'

Spider's joyous voice floated down from the crow's-nest. 'Señorita Tiggy, look, we've got us some new guides.'

Tiggy followed the line of Spider's finger. There, to the side of the sloop, was a pod of dolphins, arcing their way through the waves towards them. The grief temporarily eased as wonder filtered through her body. The dolphins reached the edge of the sloop and paused, seeming to stand upright in the water, half-smiles plastered beneath their pointed grey noses. They began to click, a sound almost like laughing.

'They want something,' Marina said.

Tiggy nodded and shouted up to the crow's-nest, 'Spider, what do you think they want?'

'I'm afraid I don't speak dolphin, though I'm fluent in jellyfish.'

She ignored his sarcastic reply and watched as the dolphins clicked excitedly, their upright bodies seeming to skip along the water, their flippers clapping like hands.

'I think they want to help us,' Marina said.

'Help how?' Miguel asked, as he and Cannon came up behind them. 'They can't exactly guide the ship like all them fish – there's only a dozen of them.'

As if in response, one of the dolphins butted right up against the side of the sloop, gripping an overhanging length of rope in its mouth.

'Oi!' Cannon shouted. 'Get off me rope, you thieving grey creature.'

'The rope!' Tiggy exclaimed. 'The dolphins want to tow the ship.' She watched as the dolphins took up position at the front of the ship, their clicks mixing with the sound of the sea.

Lucia appeared from the stern, telescope at the ready. She caught Tiggy's eye and grinned. 'Crew,' she bellowed. 'I need some rope, on the double.'

'Twelve pieces,' Marina added helpfully.

The decks buzzed with life as the crew busied themselves tying the ropes to the wooden railings at the bow of the ship. Tiggy and Marina checked the strength of each knot, before hurling the cords as hard as they could into the water below.

Each dolphin gripped a rope end between their pearly teeth and began to pull. The sloop juddered forwards and the dolphins began to swim, their gleaming bodies rearing from the water like a team of horses. The *Resolute* accepted its new fate, gathering speed and altering course accordingly; a carriage drawn by dolphins.

'Yo ho ho,' Lucia cried, excitement causing her voice to shine.

'Yo ho ho,' the crew shouted back, punching fists into the air and slapping each other on the back; even Tiggy and Marina joined in, loving the way it rolled from their tongues.

Lucia raised her telescope to her eye, wincing as the metal nudged the scar on her cheek. 'Still nothing. Just open sea.' She tucked the spyglass into her belt and eyed Tiggy and Marina sideways. 'This be some strange ocean magic, lasses.' She smiled. 'Come, get some food, you've eaten nothing since you boarded, and those sea legs won't last on air alone.'

'Food,' Cannon cheered.

Marina and Tiggy followed Lucia to the helm of the ship, Miguel and Cannon close behind. They passed Doc, who leant against the wheel, the breeze lifting a sheen of grog from his skin.

'Captain,' he muttered.

'We'll grab some food, then you and Spider can eat,' Lucia replied.

He nodded, unable to stop the relief surfacing on his rum-pinkened face.

They ducked through a low wooden doorway and entered what Tiggy presumed was the captain's cabin, right at the back of the ship. It was a small room which smelt of damp wood and cooked fish, and was decorated with drawings of unimaginable sea beasts and maps. Most of the glass panes lining the windows at the back were cracked or yellowed; indeed, everything in the room had faded, though it offered the memory of something more luxurious.

Were Padre's quarters similar to this? Tiggy had always imagined them to be larger, plusher, though now – along with him – they were buried at the bottom of the ocean. She clenched her throat, trying to prevent the tears from working their way towards her eyes.

She sat on a green velvet chair, several of which encircled a small, rickety table. The cabin clearly wasn't used to accommodating so many people, so Cannon had to make do with an upturned barrel. Miguel laid out some hard tack – the dry biscuits which haunted the diet of many a poor sailor – and some of the ham and bread Tiggy had taken from her pantry. Cannon began slopping an off-white, lumpy, foul-smelling liquid into some glasses, then proceeded to lick a drizzle from her hand.

'Thanks for bringing this,' Lucia said, stuffing a piece of ham in her mouth. Cannon and Miguel followed suit, and soon only a few flecks of pink remained. 'Normally it's just hard tack and any fish we've managed to catch,' Lucia mumbled whilst she chewed.

Tiggy and Marina both faltered; they were raised with the manners of the Islanders, so when nobody offered them anything, they tentatively snaffled a hunk of bread each before all that was left was hard tack and crumbs.

'Leave some for Doc and Spider,' Lucia said.

Tiggy flushed; she'd only taken one bite, yet she put the hunk back and settled on a piece of hard tack. It looked like a slither of rock – hard and full of cracks.

Miguel grabbed her wrist before she could lift the morsel to her mouth. 'I would highly recommend you knock it first, Señorita Tiggy.' Gently, he guided her hand so it banged the biscuit against the table. Several maggots fell from the cracks and tumbled on to the table top.

Marina let out a small yelp of disgust.

But Tiggy forced herself to smile. 'Thanks,' she told Miguel, before taking a tiny nibble of the rock. It tasted of mould and felt like chalk, seeming to suck all the moisture from her mouth. She ordered her stomach not to heave, her mouth to chew, and somehow, she managed to swallow without even a grimace. She wanted to feel like part of the crew, like a real pirate, even if it meant gnawing on a maggot's leftovers. After several more bites, she knocked back her drink. It felt like frogspawn against her tongue and tasted like gone-off cheese. She began to cough.

Cannon laughed and slapped her on the back. 'If you can eat hard tack, you're a true pirate in my book.'

A beaming smile, which no amount of coughing could dislodge, spread across Tiggy's face. 'What did I just drink?' she asked. 'Is that a special pirate drink?'

'Nah, that be goat's milk,' Cannon replied.

'That was milk?' Tiggy said, trying not to retch.

Cannon nodded with pride. 'Aged like a fine wine.'

'I thought pirates drank rum,' Marina said.

Lucia shook her head. 'We don't drink and sail.'

Tiggy wasn't sure if Doc had got that message yet.

Grinning, Miguel raised his glass of congealed milk. 'Leaping starfish, am I glad to be a pirate again.'

Cannon mirrored him, sloshing milk on to her lap. 'Yo ho ho to that.'

'The *Resolute* weren't built for trading,' Lucia said.

'And I weren't built for fishing,' Cannon said, glancing at the knives which hung from her belt.

'To treasure,' Miguel roared, gulping down his lumpy milk as if it were no more than water.

'To treasure,' Lucia and Cannon shouted, following suit.

Tiggy raised her glass. 'And saving our brothers from an evil mage,' she added.

Lucia wiped her mouth with the back of her hand. 'Well, it seems you weren't kidding about that mermaid friend of yours.'

'No, Captain,' Tiggy replied.

'I'm sorry we doubted you, Antigua,' Lucia said, and the crew nodded their agreement.

'That's OK,' she replied.

'And it's important we don't keep secrets from each other, don't you think?' Lucia arched an eyebrow and left a meaningful pause.

'What do you mean?' Tiggy asked.

'Back on the pier . . .' The captain wriggled both brows. 'We heard what Gabriella told you about the Bloodmoon prophecy.'

The words ignited a spark of fear in Tiggy's stomach and her smile dropped. 'Oh, *that*,' she said. Sitting in the captain's quarters, eating tack, pretending to be a pirate, she'd managed to block out her brother's fate for a moment or two – the act of remembering sickened her more than the clotted goat's milk. 'I'm afraid I don't know anything other than what you heard. There's some prophecy called the Bloodmoon prophecy, and the mermaid has probably told it to the mage.'

Lucia crossed her heart. 'Kraken, save us,' she whispered.

'Do you think Gabriella's right, then?' Tiggy asked. 'That the new mage wants to reawaken the curse of Haven? I mean, I never really knew if the curse was real or just a story.'

The collective inhalation of shock from Lucia, Miguel and Cannon filled the cabin. 'Sweet Kraken,' Cannon whispered. 'And with the Bloodmoon tomorrow. Shame on you, Antigua.'

'Me neither,' Marina said, rushing to her friend's defence. 'I mean, nobody really knows, do they?

Anyone who survived it is long dead.'

Miguel glanced around the room as if the walls had ears. 'You shouldn't speak so, Seňorita Marina. What those boys went through, it should be honoured, remembered, not cast in doubt.'

Marina offered an apologetic smile. 'We believed the boys were stolen, of course. We just thought maybe they were sold into slavery or something a little more . . . realistic.'

'And what's unrealistic about man abusing power?' Lucia asked. 'About man disrespecting the forces of nature.' She paused to slosh more milk into her glass. 'If you knew the true story, the real story behind the Pirate King, then you wouldn't be so ready to dismiss the curse of Haven as fantasy.'

'What story?' Tiggy asked, curiosity stirring inside.

Lucia tossed back her drink. 'When we were pirates, we heard all kinds of things. Stories the Islanders allowed to sink beneath the waves of time.'

'Please, tell us,' Tiggy begged, clutching her empty glass so hard her knuckles whitened.

Lucia glanced at Miguel and Cannon. 'What do you reckon?'

Miguel smiled. 'Anyone who can summon a pod of dolphins deserves to know, I reckon.'

Cannon nodded and muttered, 'Fire in the hole,' which Tiggy presumed meant yes.

Lucia rested her hands on the table, steadying herself against the tilt of the waves. 'Slavery wasn't enough. The Pirate King hated the people of Haven so deeply he wanted to destroy their hearts and minds. Turning the boys into Sea Golems, making them bend to his will like puppets and attack their own, wasn't just so he could control the ocean – it was to punish the Islanders.'

'Why?' Marina whispered.

Lucia dropped her voice, further shrouding her tale with intrigue. 'Once there lived a sorceress of the sea, a powerful one at that, but she decided to leave the ocean life and raise her family on land. She chose to settle on Haven, the island at the heart of the ocean, so she could still fall asleep listening to the whispering of the waves. Soon she had a little boy...'

'The Pirate King?' Marina asked.

Lucia nodded. 'Though he was just a boy before he became King.'

'So what happened to him?' Tiggy urged.

'Sea witches were not welcome on land,' Lucia said. 'And even though she used her magic for healing and calming the waves when boats came in, the Islanders put her on trial.'

Marina gasped. 'There were witch trials, here in Haven?'

'Aye, Señorita,' Miguel said. 'Magic has always scared people.'

'Tell me about it,' Marina whispered, her fingers toying with the winkle shell around her neck.

Tiggy touched her friend's arm. 'It's only 'cause they're jealous, Mari.'

Lucia continued. 'The Islanders banished the sorceress from Haven, casting her out to sea in a rickety old sloop. She was never seen again. They said she missed her son so much she died of a broken heart.'

'And the Pirate King?' Tiggy asked, ashamed by the kernel of sympathy which grew in her stomach.

'They kept him on the island; thought they were doing the right thing, giving him a normal life. But the boy didn't see it that way. Filled with rage and anger, he grew his gift for sorcery from hatred rather than love. The curse was an extension of his hatred.'

'Wow,' Tiggy said. 'No wonder the Islanders wanted to forget that story, it almost makes me feel . . .' She faltered on her words, unable to finish the sentence.

'Sorry for him?' Cannon asked.

Tiggy gave a stiff nod.

'Ha,' Cannon said, slapping a dagger on the table and causing Tiggy and Marina to flinch. 'Don't you go feeling sorry for that evil sea cucumber. It's his fault the boys were stolen. If he hadn't cast the curse in the first place, there would be no curse to resurrect tomorrow, would there?'

Cannon was right, and Tiggy felt any sympathy for the Pirate King flake away as she pictured Diego being carried away by Snake-hair. 'So who's this new mage?' she asked.

'Who knows?' Lucia said. 'Though rumour has it that the Pirate King had a child of his own, so it's possible he has relatives out there. One thing I know is that the new mage has loathing in his heart to rival the Pirate King's.'

Marina bit her lip, deep in thought. 'Your story explains why the Pirate King hated the Islanders so much, but even if he is a descendant, why does the new mage?'

Lucia shrugged. 'Maybe he doesn't. Maybe he just wants an army. Whilst the magical sea creatures remain distrustful of man, I doubt they'd unite behind an evil mage now. They lost too many of their own under the Pirate King's reign. And besides, the rift between man and the sea is easing – some mermaids actually help men lost at sea nowadays.'

'And selkies,' Marina added defensively. 'They're helpful too.'

Miguel roared with laughter. 'That sounds like something a selkie would say.'

'I'm not a selkie,' Marina said, frowning. 'Just because my madre is—' She was silenced by the door bursting open. It was Spider, looking slightly out of breath. 'Captain, the dolphins have gone.'

Lucia scraped back her chair. 'So which creatures have taken over now?'

Spider grinned. 'Just the one.' He paused, adding a touch of drama. 'A blue whale.'

The group dashed to the bow of the ship, excitement pulsing through them. But the waves were empty.

Spider was already scuttling back up the netting towards the crow's-nest; his feet snagged on the rope, yet somehow, he managed not to fall. 'Has grog-rot set into your landlubber brains already?' His laughter rang across the decks. 'You're at the wrong end.'

Tiggy, Marina and the crew dashed to the helm

and leant over the railings at the back of the sloop. Sure enough, seeming to sprout from the stern like a small island, was the back of a mighty whale. It was shunting the boat through the ocean as though it were no heavier than a tiny raft. Tiggy grabbed Marina's hand and they both began to laugh, relief and hope winding through their bodies – surely they would find their brothers now.

Cannon and Miguel cheered and the whale responded with a squirt of water, which gushed from the spout on its back like a fountain. A muted tone rumbled through the deck and into their boots.

Lucia hugged Tiggy to the side of her body. 'That mermaid of yours doesn't give up, does she?'

Tiggy grinned. *No*, she thought. *And neither will I.*

CHAPTER 20

Come dusk, the whale boomed its last goodbye and sank into the depths below. Tiggy searched the waters, eager to see what creature the ocean would provide next. At first, they were a mere twinkle in the distance, a shimmer of colour beneath the night-darkened waves, but as they neared, Tiggy realized the shimmer was in fact a swarm of bioluminescent jellyfish. She raced to the front of the sloop where they took up post, their ethereal bodies glowing like lanterns beneath the surface of the waves.

She leant over the bow, trying to get a better look, Marina and Miguel by her side. 'They're beautiful,' she gasped.

Marina reached down and swiped through the air as if she could scoop them up and study them more closely. 'I've never seen anything like it.'

'Can't stand the little critters,' Miguel said, lifting up his trouser leg to reveal a patch of pearly raised skin, only just visible in the half-light. 'They sting like the devil.'

Lucia arrived, a smile clutching her lips. 'Well I never, the perfect guide come nightfall.' She glanced at Miguel and frowned. 'Put your leg away, Miguel, it's hairier than a horse's back.'

'It's not my fault,' he grumbled, rolling down his trouser leg. 'Me head hair slid down me body soon as I hit thirty.'

They watched in silence as the ghostly beacons of hope undulated before them, every colour imaginable held within their glassy forms. And as the ocean snuffed out the final rays of the sun, the glow of the jellyfish seemed to intensify. Tiggy inhaled deeply. The sea air smelt heavier at night, dense with salt and stirring the hairs on her neck with cold and the unknown. She wondered if this was what magic tasted like. She wished Padre were beside her to enjoy it too, and that familiar hollow feeling of loss began to open inside her stomach.

Just then, the sloop passed through a shimmering wall of turquoise light. Tiggy watched in awe as it danced across her skin and passed all the way across the night-bleached planks of the *Resolute*, from bow to stern.

'Woah,' Miguel muttered.

A cry from above caught their attention. 'Land ahoy,' Spider bellowed. 'Land ahoy!'

Tiggy's head whipped up. Excitement curled through her as she anticipated a speck of land appearing in the gloom ahead, perhaps the faint glimmer of tavern windows and the more powerful shine of flares marking out a port. But instead, the sight filled her with shock, every one of her muscles transforming to stone. A small island loomed in the darkness before them – a giant fin of volcanic rock rearing from the waves. It was so close. How had they only seen it now? It was as if it had appeared from *nowhere*. Fear encircled her chest, pushing a small scream into the night.

The eyeglass slipped from Lucia's fingers and clattered against the wood. 'Sweet Kraken,' she whispered under her breath. 'I've heard of the merfolk concealing things from the eyes of man . . . corals, treasures and alike . . . but an entire island?'

'You think the merfolk did this?' Miguel asked.

Lucia shook her head. 'I suspect we've found our mage.'

'So the boys are here too?' Tiggy asked, her yearning causing her voice to tremble. 'Diego and Felipe?'

'Where else better to hide a hundred stolen boys than on a secret island?' Lucia replied.

'Well, come on then.' Tiggy's words tripped over each other. 'We can dock in no time.'

'No.' Lucia gazed at the mysterious island ahead. 'We won't be able to navigate the rocks in the dark, Antigua. It'll be too risky. Best circle here for the night and approach in the morning.'

Marina frowned. 'Wouldn't it make more sense to approach at night? The last thing we want is to be seen, as we'd lose the element of surprise.'

'We don't know the rocks,' Lucia replied. 'We could rip the stern if we're not careful.'

Tiggy was about to blurt out that she didn't care if they ripped the stern (it was only a ship, after all) when Lucia added, 'And then how will we escape.

Besides, we've got time. The Bloodmoon isn't until tomorrow night.'

Spider's voice drifted down towards them. 'You're forgetting, I'm fluent in jellyfish.'

'Now's not the time, Spider,' Miguel scolded, glancing at Tiggy's miserable expression.

But Spider merely laughed. 'Seriously, Captain. Look into the water.'

Lucia clutched the railings and leant towards the water below. Her face shone with childlike wonder, any shadows of doubt banished from her features in an instant. 'Oh, Spider!' she exclaimed. 'I do believe you're right. They're guiding us between the rocks.'

Tiggy watched as the jellyfish switched direction to dodge a nasty-looking crag. She felt lighter, as if a huge weight had lifted from her chest. She looked at Marina, barely able to contain the joy in her voice. 'We're so close, Mari.'

Maybe it was the moonlight or the seasickness, but Marina didn't look so sure.

'What is it?' Tiggy asked.

'I don't know,' Marina replied. 'It just seems a bit easy.'

Tiggy nudged her friend playfully in the ribs. 'We've survived a giant squid, a pirate raid and sailed unchartered waters with the help of the sea . . . easy is not a word I'd choose.'

'You're probably right.' But Marina's smile didn't reach her eyes.

CHAPTER 21

Clara flopped into the underground river below. The salt water was so fresh it seemed to sparkle against her skin and fizz through her gills, reducing the fatigue and hunger to a distant memory. She felt so rejuvenated, so joyful, she momentarily forgot about the boy who had rescued her, even as he splashed and flailed beside her, holding his breath and trying to figure out which way was up. She even forgot about the evil sorcerer who would no doubt follow them at any moment. All she could think about was how good it felt to stretch her tail. To be free.

A pain shot up her scales as Felipe's hands desperately scrabbled up her tailfin. She snapped back to reality and pulled the boy upright so his head surfaced, allowing him to inhale a greedy lungful of air.

'It's OK,' she told him. 'Just breathe.' She glanced around. They were in some sort of underground cave system, a series of tunnels which presumably spread beneath the island like a network of arteries. A crisp plate of light shone from the rock above like a small sun – it was the hole they had fallen through only moments ago, the rusted pipe still pointing straight into the water below.

Suddenly the mage's head appeared in the hole above, crowned by light and pinched with hate. 'Do you really think you can escape me?' His voice echoed around the tunnel like a thunderclap.

Clara's stomach cramped with anxiety as she watched the mage's face flicker in a turquoise glow. She imagined him carving some hateful image in the air above and thrusting it towards her, pouring a lifetime of pain into her body. One thing was certain, she wasn't sticking around to discover which means of torture was next on his list. So with Felipe's hand firmly clutched in her own, she flicked her tail and shot into the dark maze of tunnels, deep into the heart of the island.

After a while, Clara glanced over her shoulder. 'Are you OK?'

'Yes,' he spluttered, slicing his arms through the water and following in her wake. Even after his accident, he was a strong swimmer. Her tail was the only light source in the underground caves; it cast a purple blaze into the pool around them and on to the dome of rock above. Felipe was sure her tail shone brighter than when in the tank, perhaps because the ocean gave her strength.

Eventually they reached a bigger cave with several water-filled tunnels branching off. It felt like a large, watery grave – dimly lit, the stench of fish, rock and damp moss heavy in their nostrils, yet Felipe was starting to tire and so indicated to Clara he needed to rest. It was hard to tell how long they'd been swimming without seeing the course of the sun across the sky, but it felt like hours. He found the rocky bottom with his foot, steadied himself with outstretched hands and took a moment to catch his breath.

'Your leg healed well, I see.' An awkward smile gripped Clara's mouth.

Felipe noticed that even though her teeth were sharp and pointed, she still looked prettier when she smiled. He nodded. 'Yes, thanks to you.' Sometimes when he closed his eyes, he could still feel the magic leaching from her fingers into the wound from where his lower leg had been ripped from him. She had stemmed the blood flow, sealed the vessels and prevented infection with the mere press of her hand. Her padre had then carried him through the waves back to Haven, risking being seen by the Islanders just so he could deliver the wounded boy back home. Felipe's eyes itched with the thought of it and he had to blink back his tears. 'Why did you help me?' Though no more than a whisper, his voice sounded loud, bouncing back at him from the cavern walls. 'I never got to ask. You simply told me your names, and then vanished.'

'The feud between the sea and man still exists, but Madre taught me that it should not define us.' Her eyes filled with tears at the thought of her darling madre. 'I am a mermaid. I use my magic to protect and heal both sea creatures and man alike, Felipe – just like it always was before the Pirate King stirred up hatred between us, encouraging us to focus on our differences rather than what unites us.'

Hearing his name on her lips surprised him. She had remembered it, even after all this time. 'If you and your padre hadn't arrived when you did, that shark would surely have finished off the rest of me.'

'Hush. We were there, and you're fine now . . . apart from being kidnapped by an evil mage, that is.'

Felipe laughed in spite of himself. He had so many questions, so much he needed to talk about, but all he could do was marvel at the purple scales gleaming from the sides of her face. She was magical . . . *amazing*. Why did humans hate merfolk so? Was it simply because of the past, because of the Pirate King? Or were they still scared of difference? He inhaled the dank, briny air and settled on just one more question. 'Why were you in that tank?'

Her features tightened, a combination of fear, sorrow and something Felipe couldn't quite place. Shame, perhaps? He instantly regretted the question. 'It's OK . . .' he stammered. 'I . . . I didn't mean to upset you.'

She sniffed loudly. 'It's fine. It's a perfectly sensible thing to ask.' She paused, glancing around their cave, suddenly mindful of the steady drip of water, the lack of light, the whereabouts of the hateful mage and his cronies. 'I'll tell you later, but now we should keep on moving. Who knows what that mage is capable of? Once we reach open water, we'll be safe and I'll take you back to Haven, then we can lead the Islanders to the boys before the Bloodmoon.' She gestured to her back. 'You can climb on board if you're tired.'

'Thanks,' Felipe said, hauling himself on to Clara's back.

He felt her push through the water like a powerful sloop, leaving the cavern behind and heading down a narrow tunnel.

CHAPTER 22

The jellyfish led the *Resolute* towards the secret island, navigating the crags of rock which emerged from the darkness like monstrous gravestones. The captain was right – without their shining guides, a ripped stern would have been a certainty.

As they neared the land mass, Tiggy could see a volcano at its very peak, a stark barb silhouetted against the soft smudge of night stars. Towards the beaches, the rock was stippled with foliage, grey and sparkling beneath the light of the moon, though she imagined it would turn emerald beneath the sun. She squinted and could just pick out the shape of a grand castle peering from the island's rocky terrain, its turrets seeming to twist upwards more like giant trees than something built from stone. Could it be the mage's home? Were Diego, Felipe and the rest of the boys locked in its dungeons? She imagined them scared and trapped, and her heart ached.

The island loomed closer and the crags became more treacherous, clustering together so that they looked like giant hands, their spiky fingers just waiting to grab at the sloop. Lucia ordered they drop the sail and pick up the oars to slow their approach.

Whilst scrabbling to find an oar, Marina caught Tiggy by the arm. 'I still can't believe it's this easy,' she whispered. 'He goes to all the effort of conceal-ing his island from passing ships, and then we're able to land with no trouble.'

Tiggy smiled and rested a soothing hand on her friend's arm. 'Maybe he thought the rocks would put people off.'

'Rocks? Sounds a bit tame for a villainous mage.'

'You worry too much, Mari. Look, we're nearly there.'

But as they looked towards the island, they saw

something impossible and terrifying on the surface of the water. Strands of turquoise light appeared on top of the waves, like giant blue flames flickering in the night. The strands morphed and shifted, snaking in the wind, gaining clarity and shape with every second.

The crew dropped their oars and Tiggy and Marina clung to each other. A distant rumble sounded around them and the air filled with the stench of copper and rotting fish. Tiggy watched in horror – too afraid to speak, let alone breathe – as the ghostly strands began to take human form. Hundreds of men and women, built from a shimmering blue-green light and hovering between the sloop and the beach.

Spider climbed down from the crow's-nest and joined them. 'The Army of Lost Souls . . . souls lost at sea.' Terror caused his words to shake.

'But . . . but . . .' Marina stammered. 'I thought the lost souls were all held safely in Davy Jones's locker.'

'Most of them are,' he said. 'But a powerful mage can bewitch the souls of men who've fallen at his own hand.'

She observed the ghostly figures. Judging from their dress, they were a collection of sea folk –

soldiers, pirates, sailors, fishermen – and they all wore upon their bodies the tales of their grizzly deaths. Holes carved from bullets, knives still embedded in skulls and necks, missing arms and legs. One pirate had a huge shark bite taken out of him, and some were simply wrapped in seaweed and barnacles, a sign the ocean had claimed the air from their lungs and that their real bodies still lay at the bottom of the sea. The mage had been busy, it seemed.

Tiggy felt sick. 'Ghosts, Golems, a giant squid...' she murmured, her breath uncurling into the night. 'Is there anything the mage can't control?'

'Can they harm us?' Marina asked in a small voice. 'I mean, surely they can't actually touch anything. They're *ghosts*.'

Lucia nodded, her face grave. 'They don't need to touch us to harm us, Marina.'

'What do you mean?' she replied.

'The Army of Lost Souls relive their death again and again, releasing a horrific noise known in legend as a Death Echo.'

'And the Death Echo, does it . . . it . . . hurt?' Marina whispered.

Lucia marched to the bow of the ship. 'May I

suggest we don't stick around to find out. Crew, take up your oars, prepare to man the sails.'

But everyone stood motionless, watching the figures in horror. The rumbling climbed, the stench increased, and slowly, purposefully, the ghouls began to move towards them, their step so firm it was as if they were unaware they walked on water. A terrifying thought speared Tiggy's heart: Could her padre be amongst them? Her lungs froze and her heart missed a beat, her eyes desperately scanning the tortured faces of the approaching ghouls. Yet there was no sign of Padre.

'Oi!' Lucia roared. 'Call yourself pirates or a bunch of useless landlubbers. Take to the oars. Raise the sails. NOW!'

But before the crew could move, before they could lift the rigging and raise any sail, the Army of Lost Souls began to storm towards the ship, their faces twisting as they released a collective battle cry and raised their ghostly weapons high.

Tiggy's hands flew to her mouth, adrenalin bursting through her veins.

'Cannon,' Captain roared. 'Try the cannons, you never know.'

No reply.

'She's taking a nap,' Miguel replied.

'Typical,' Lucia muttered. She turned to the crew, her face alive with excitement. 'Batten down the hatches, grab your weapons, and remember . . .' She raised her voice and punched her fist in the air. 'Dead men tell no tales.'

What if they're already dead? Tiggy thought.

The ship hummed with life, crew members hurriedly passing around rifles and blades, desperately trying to weaponize before the Army of Lost Souls reached the deck. Through the darkness, the panic, the wails of the approaching ghosts, and the click of ammunition slotting into barrels, Tiggy felt Miguel's hand land on her shoulder. 'Tiggy, Marina, go to the crew's quarters and lock the door.'

Marina was already dashing towards the stairs at the bow of the ship, but Tiggy hung back. 'I can fight,' she said, ashamed at how her body quaked.

Miguel shook his head, the gold of his earring almost silver – at first Tiggy assumed it was the moonlight, then she realized the entire night sky was cast in the aqua glow of the ghost army. 'No way,' he said firmly. 'It ain't safe.'

Before she could object, the ship trembled so violently she was almost thrown to the floor. She steadied herself against Marina and watched in horror as a hundred ghostly fingers curled over the side of the sloop. It was too late to hide. Flickering blue figures began launching themselves over the sides of the ship, landing on the deck with muted thuds. Marina screamed and Tiggy felt her knees buckle.

At least a dozen spirits now stood on the deck, with more arriving with every second – it was like watching a horde of ants engulf a small hill. The crew jumped into action. Lucia began to fire, Spider pointed his sword and Miguel ran towards them with a raised club. But the weapons merely passed through the invaders' translucent bodies as if they were built from air.

Tiggy and Marina clung to each other, their chests heaving, their legs shaking; this close, Tiggy could make out every line and scar on the glowing faces of the apparitions. She grabbed a nearby oar and began to swing, keeping Marina behind her at all times. Unsurprisingly, the paddle was as useless as the crew's weapons.

'Tiggy, look,' Marina whispered, her voice pulled rigid and cracking with fear.

The wraiths had frozen. A tense silence coated

the air. Then, moving as one, they threw back their heads, opened their mouths and released a wail of unspeakable pain into the night.

The Death Echo.

Tiggy's hands flew to her ears, but there was no escaping the sound as it swelled inside her head like an angry tumour. Misery grew and grew until it began to overwhelm her, so much so, that her legs began to buckle and her vision began to wane. The screams climbed higher, speaking not just of physical pain, but of the injustice of lives cut short: the music that would never be danced to, the feasts left uneaten, the sunshine which could never warm their faces. The Death Echo crescendoed into a final unitary note of desolation, filled with every family left behind, every sweetheart left unloved, of torture and loss and the end of possibilities.

It was unbearable. And one by one, the crew dropped to their knees, covering their faces and sobbing, reliving every moment of death alongside the poor, lost souls.

Tiggy desperately wanted to help, but the Death Echo pushed inside her soul and dragged every last shred of hope and joy from her. Her body began to crumble and, in her final moments of lucidity,

Padre's kind face filled her mind. 'Padre,' she whispered. 'My darling padre.'

Above the Death Echo, above the pain, she heard a thin voice. 'Tiggy, my necklace, look at my necklace.'

Tiggy forced open her eyes and squinted through the haze of despair. Marina lay beside her, the winkle shell around her neck glowing a brilliant turquoise blue.

CHAPTER 23

'For you are born of a wave,' Tiggy whispered, remembering Gabriella's words.

As if in response, they heard a female voice, singing from beyond the ship. It was a note so pure, it seemed to cut through the waves, the fear and the confusion, and meet the Death Echo head-on. The two conflicting sounds battled for space – beauty versus anguish, peace versus horror – and eventually, the Death Echo seemed to fade, as if soothed by a healing balm.

The single pure note bent into a wondrous melody

which twisted around the deck like a butterfly. Tiggy's mouth fell open. It was the most beautiful song she had ever heard, and though she hadn't a clue who the voice belonged to, she let her eyes glaze over, allowing all the loss and anguish to evaporate.

Another exquisite, female voice joined from beyond the ship, then another, and another. Soon, a choir sang in perfect unison. It took Tiggy a second to realize that one of the voices belonged to her best friend. Marina's necklace blazed as she sang, her eyes closed in rapture.

As the Death Echo dwindled, the phantoms began lowering their heads and blinking in surprise. Tiggy felt her strength return and, shakily, began to stand. The crew followed suit, rubbing their aching ears and wiping the tears from their eyes. Eventually, the Death Echo sputtered out completely.

'Look . . .' Spider whispered.

The spirits before them began to sway on the spot; their eyelids fluttered as the final drops of desolation drained from their faces entirely. And one by one, the spirits dissolved in a haze of turquoise light.

Only when the last soul vanished did the singing stop. The light in Marina's necklace extinguished and she slumped to the ground, exhausted. Tiggy and Miguel scooped her into a sitting position. She was pale, but her breathing was strong.

Doc checked the pulse in her wrist. 'She'll be fine,' he said kindly. 'She just needs rest. I'm guessing she hasn't used her powers before?'

'I don't think she even knew about them,' Tiggy replied.

'Captain.' Spider leant over the railings, his voice both amazed and scared. 'Them be selkies in the waters.'

Tiggy moved beside Spider and peered into the gloom. She could just make out the heads of a dozen seals bobbing in the sea beside them, each one with a tiny winkle shell glowing around their necks.

'Why are the selkies helping us suddenly?' Spider asked.

Lucia joined them. 'The necklace summoned them. Maybe now Marina will accept that she's a selkie too.'

'I'm not a—' Marina weakly began to object, when a voice, smooth with confidence, spoke from the helm of the ship. 'Greetings, travellers. I am Susana.'

They spun to see a tall woman walking towards them. She wore a simple red dress, a long grey cloak and a calm expression. Her brown skin glistened with sea water and her black hair fell in a wet sheet across her shoulders. Clutched in her hands was a large grey bundle, which sparkled in the light of the moon. A blue-green winkle charm glowed around her neck.

'What are you doing so close to the Mefisto Island?' she asked. 'There's a reason it's hidden. It belongs to *him*.'

Lucia stepped forward, signifying her position as captain. 'Do you mean the mage? The one who controls that poor squid?'

Susana nodded firmly.

'What does he want with the boys?' Tiggy asked, even though the answer scared her.

Susana eyed her up and down. 'Antigua de Fortune. You are just how I imagined, if a little shorter.'

'How do you know my name?' Tiggy asked.

Susana smiled knowingly.

Tiggy opened her mouth, her thoughts muddying with confusion, but Susana cut across her. 'And this must be Gabriella's daughter.' She gestured to Marina, whose eyes were now partway open. 'Selkie blood and born of a wave.'

Marina managed a feeble, 'Yes.'

'You look just like your madre. She must be very proud,' Susana said.

Marina forced a shy smile.

Tiggy suddenly felt like an imposter. All she'd done was hear the voice of a mermaid. Marina was the one with ocean magic, not her.

Lucia gestured to the ship and the sea beyond. 'What happened to the Army of Lost Souls?'

Susana moved towards them. She had a face which was hard and kind all at once, magic etched into every feature. 'The mage stopped those poor spirits from reaching their final resting place so they could guard his precious island. He used his sorcery to strip them of all hope and joy, leaving them only with the memory of their tragic deaths. When we sang, we relieved them of the hatred which bound them to this earth, so finally they could cross into Davy Jones's locker.'

'So you didn't just save us?' Tiggy said. 'You saved them too.'

Susana smiled. 'Indeed.' She held the grey bundle towards Marina. It looked like a grey coat rolled up.

'What is it?' Marina asked, her words slightly slurred. 'Madre has one just like it.'

'You have earnt your sealskin, Marina. Travelling

across the ocean to save your brother, using your shell to protect your friends and summon your shoal.'

Marina took the bundle and let it unroll to its full length. It was a large cape, just like Susana's, which shimmered in the starlight and smelt of the sea. The crew gasped and Tiggy fought the urge to clutch her friend excitedly by the arm.

'Keep it safe, for without it you will be unable to transform.' Susana then gestured to the necklace around Marina's neck. 'And your charm, keep it on you always, for a selkie's magic will not work without it.' She pointed to a twisting, organic building which sat in the distance. 'The mage has a castle, grown from the island itself. You will find your brothers there, I believe.'

'How do you know . . . ?' Tiggy tailed off, suddenly unsure if she should trust the selkie before her.

She smiled. 'Why, the same way the creatures of the sea knew where to find you. We talk to each other. We listen to the waves.'

'Waves don't talk,' Spider muttered.

'Maybe you don't know how to listen,' Susana replied. She turned to Tiggy. 'Good luck, Antigua. I will be rooting for you.' And with that, she ran towards the side of the sloop and threw herself from the deck. Mid-air, she wrapped the cloak around her, arcing towards the water like a giant moth inside a cocoon. It happened fast, but Tiggy swore the cloak melded into Susana's skin, becoming part of her, so that when the selkie hit the waves, she had already transformed into another glossy-coated seal.

Everyone turned to stare at Marina, mouths agog, eyes wide.

Ever so slowly, she shrugged. 'Well then . . . I guess that makes me a selkie.'

And with that, she fainted.

CHAPTER 24

Clara could feel the current of the ocean strengthening against her scales as they neared the open water; the sea breeze and the sound of the waves seemed to draw her from the tunnels like a splinter.

'We're nearly there,' she told her passenger.

They reached an opening in the side of the island and swam into a pool of exposed water. The starstrewn sky stretched above and the sound of darkness embraced them – crickets and the soft hum of the ocean.

Felipe began to laugh, enjoying the sight of the moon. 'You did it,' he whispered.

'Almost, there're some hefty mangroves to get through.' She pointed at the mesh of low-hanging trees and salt water rivers which stretched between them and the ocean. It was a touch frustrating, but at least she could see the sky and the ember of the ocean at night, holding in its blackened waves the reflection of the stars and the promise of freedom.

Felipe unravelled from her back and, side by side, they began to slip between tree roots and small sandy bays. The canopy of leaves caused the moon to waver like a trembling, white flame.

Clara turned to the boy. 'When we reach Haven' – her voice broke for a second – 'tell them I am so very sorry.'

'Sorry for what?' Felipe asked, using a low-hanging branch to propel himself forwards. 'What were you doing in that tank, Clara?'

She dunked her head underwater for a moment, letting the salt water rinse away her tears. When she surfaced, she spoke in a low, soft voice. 'The raid, the kidnapping . . . they were my fault.'

'What do you mean . . . your fault?'

Clara gazed at him. She had to tell him. The guilt

was gnawing at her insides with no signs of relenting. She took a deep breath. 'I told the mage the prophecy of the Bloodmoon.'

Felipe shook his head. 'What prophecy? What are you talking about?'

Her body suddenly felt too heavy to float. She imagined just sinking into her lovely ocean and hiding from the world above. From the mage and the boys and Felipe's dark eyes. She could just swim away and leave it all behind, find her family and never think of the eels and her terrible betrayal again. Her tail began to flick with excitement. But she scolded it silently. *Not yet. First, we must put things right.*

She laid a hand on Felipe's shoulder. 'The prophecy of the Bloodmoon is the ocean's most dangerous prophecy, born from the death of the Pirate King and protected all these years by the merfolk.'

Felipe tried to smile. 'Come now, it can't be *that* bad. What is it?'

'I . . . I don't think I should tell you. It's a secret.'

'Well, you've already told the mage. What harm can it do?'

Clara couldn't deny his logic, and began to wonder if Felipe could actually help. At the very least, sharing it with Felipe might lighten her load a little. She took a deep breath . . .

'Beneath the Bloodmoon, the curse shall be saved,
An army of Golems shall rise from the grave,
When a child of Haven, born of a wave,
Falls at the hand of the deadliest Mage.'

The pair bobbed in silence for a moment. 'OK,' Felipe eventually said. 'That's pretty bad.'

Clara nodded. 'It means that if the mage finds the right child, the child from the prophecy, and sacrifices them beneath the Bloodmoon, then he can turn you all into Sea Golems. And now he knows.'

'That's why he wanted you to look at us back at the castle. He wanted you to identify the child from the prophecy.'

'Yes. But he must never find out who it is, Felipe. It would be disastrous.'

'Agreed.'

And they pushed through the water, leaving the treacherous island behind.

CHAPTER 25

The *Resolute* finally docked in a small bay, far from the castle and hidden from any prying eyes. Their job complete, the jellyfish floated back into the deeper waters – a cloud of balloons released into the sky. Tiggy and Doc sat on upturned barrels in the crew's quarters and watched over Marina as she slept in a hammock. Cannon still snoozed nearby, her fingers twitching as though searching for a gun she'd never fire.

'Marina's just tired,' Doc said, pushing his locs from his face and securing his red bandanna. 'Give her a few hours and she'll be ready for stage two of your adventure.'

Tiggy gazed at the hammock as it swayed in time to the waves. It was strangely relaxing, like watching the pendulum of a clock. 'I don't even know what stage two is . . . I mean, how are we supposed to rescue the boys with all that sorcery and all those pirates. There's only seven of us.' It was the first time Tiggy had voiced this concern, and saying it out loud made her insides wither.

'Aye,' Doc said, opening a flask of grog. 'And our so-called weapons expert can't keep her eyes open.' He glanced at Cannon and took a large swig from the flask. 'Mind, I'm one to talk – a doctor who's never been to school.'

'Is this supposed to make me feel better?' Tiggy asked, her belly squirming with anxiety.

His face fell. 'See. I've even got a terrible bedside manner.'

Tiggy rested a hand on his arm. 'Sorry, Doc, your bedside manner is great, really.'

'Should rename it hammock-side manner really, as I ain't seen a bed in years.' He took another long slurp of grog. ''Ere, speaking of beds, why don't you catch some shut-eye too? Captain says we ain't going nowhere till Marina's had a few hours' sleep. Says we need her at her best.'

'Why?'

Doc grinned. 'Who else is gonna sing them pesky pirates to sleep once we get on that island?'

Tiggy was embarrassed she hadn't thought of this herself – of course, they could use Marina's powers to help rescue the boys. She suppressed a flash of jealousy; she so wished she had selkie powers too. A life as a seal would be a grand life indeed.

'Come on,' Doc said kindly. 'I ain't no selkie, but I bet I can sing you off to sleep.'

Relieved to have more of a plan than she did a minute ago, Tiggy fell into a nearby hammock and closed her eyes. She realized how exhausted she was; her body swung to and fro like a lead weight and her thoughts immediately hazed together as she let Doc's voice coax her towards the land of dreams.

'Set a course for riches untold,
For buried treasure and fists of gold,
With grog in my belly and a yo ho ho,
Drop the sail and away we go.'

Tiggy's final thought before falling asleep was

that as the ship's medic, Doc should really be singing about fruit, vegetables and regular exercise, but she never got to tell him this, because she was already falling into a web of dreams.

She opened her eyes to see Spider shaking her, his face an urgent stare. 'Come look,' he whispered. 'We got us some company.'

Rubbing her eyes, Tiggy woke Marina and Cannon and followed Spider up the stairs. She reached the deck and saw Lucia, standing at the side of the sloop, eyeglass pressed to her face. The captain looked serious, her back so straight it reminded Tiggy of her padre. She ordered her eyes to remain dry. Now was not the time.

Miguel pressed a finger against his lips. 'Pirates,' he whispered.

Tiggy leant against the planks and saw movement in the distance, specks of light illuminating several figures which wound their way down the cliffs towards the mangroves. 'Do you think they've seen us?' she whispered, trying desperately to dampen the fear in her words.

Lucia lowered the telescope and shook her head. 'Not yet. But it's only a matter of time.'

'What do we do?' Tiggy asked.

'We need to abandon the *Resolute*,' Lucia replied. 'Before they spot us and attack.'

'But then we'll never escape the island,' Tiggy said, remembering Lucia's own words when she'd worried about the rocks ripping the stern.

Lucia tucked her eyeglass into her belt. 'We'll just have to steal one of their boats then.'

'Can we please pinch one that's better than this sack of old bones,' Spider whispered.

Miguel clipped him around the ear. 'Shut it. Ship's got feelings too, you know.'

'We better hurry,' Lucia said. 'There's more of them arriving.'

And then Tiggy saw him. Before anyone else. From this distance, she couldn't make out his features, but she recognized his arrogant stride and the ball of sea-green magic poised between his hands.

She swallowed, and the fear stung her throat. 'The mage is here.'

CHAPTER 26

Felipe and Clara were almost clear of the mangroves. Felipe's arms were aching, his head felt woozy and he couldn't remember a time he'd ever felt so hungry. But Clara had promised him a feast of fish as soon as they reached the ocean, and this seemed to motivate him even more than the thought of returning home.

Felipe saw the sloop nodding in the shallow waters in a bay, just visible from the edge of the mangroves. He clung on to a nearby root and peered through the leaves of a laurel. In the light of the moon, he could just pick out the rickety form of the *Resolute*. 'That ship looks familiar.'

Clara paused behind him, clearly annoyed at the interruption when they were so close to her beloved sea. 'It probably belongs to the pirates.'

Felipe shook his head. 'I recognize it from the port back at Haven.' He altered course, slipping through the water and trying to get a better view, curiosity lending him a sudden burst of strength. He could hear Clara tutting behind him, but she followed all the same.

As they gained a better view, Felipe gasped. 'Clara, look. There on the deck. That's my friend, Tiggy.'

But Clara was too busy looking at the pirates appearing at the top of the cliff, lanterns and cutlasses clasped between their hands. The sight of the mage forced a shiver through her, causing the water to lap against her chest. She clamped a watery hand over Felipe's mouth before he could call out to Tiggy, and then gestured with her head towards the figures in the distance.

Felipe saw the mage and the pirates, and nodded, fear crunching in his guts.

They watched in silence, peering over a sturdy

root as the men began to wind their way down the cliff.

'What do you think they're doing here?' Felipe eventually whispered.

'Looking for us, I imagine,' Clara replied.

Felipe glanced back to the sloop. Anxiety caused his vision to distort, yet he still recognized Lucia and the ramshackle gang from the equally ramshackle *Resolute*, a bit of a joke amongst the sailors of Haven, capable only of catching fish and never the treasure they so clearly craved, but a decent bunch all the same. What were they doing here? What was *Tiggy* doing here? His heart dropped in his chest – was his sister here too? One thing was certain: they didn't stand a chance against the mage and his men.

'Clara, we have to do something,' Felipe whispered. 'If the mage catches them, he'll kill them.'

Clara gazed longingly at the ocean. 'What can we do? There's only two of us.'

'We create a diversion,' Felipe said.

Clara shook her head. 'No way. I'm not risking getting caught again.'

Felipe clutched her hand, his face both serious and eager. 'But we have to save my friends. Come on, once we've lured them from the sloop, we can still escape.'

But Clara didn't look convinced.

'Please,' Felipe said.

She stifled a sigh. 'Fine, but just a distraction, then we make a swift exit. Agreed?'

'Agreed.'

Quickly, she dragged Felipe through the mangroves, away from the sloop and towards the other side of the cliff. Felipe watched, drenched with sea water and terror, as the pirates neared the *Resolute*.

'Now,' he told Clara.

She opened her lungs and released a blood-curdling scream.

The noise drove a blade through Felipe's head, but he didn't care. It had worked. The pirates on the cliff stopped dead in their tracks.

'More,' he whispered to her. She rolled her eyes and then shouted in her loudest voice. 'My fin. My fin is stuck, somebody help.' She then turned to Felipe and hissed, 'As if my fin would ever get stuck.'

Felipe watched as the pirates turned away from the *Resolute* and began racing towards the mangroves where he and Clara hid. 'Thank you,' he told her. 'Now come on, we can lead the pirates even further away if we keep moving.'

But Clara wasn't looking at Felipe. She was staring at the sloop, her mouth agape.

'What is it?' Felipe asked.

'It's the girl,' Clara whispered, staring at Tiggy and blinking quickly as though she didn't believe her own eyes. 'She found me! She actually found me.'

CHAPTER 27

Tiggy watched the pirates, who were already halfway down the cliffs, and it looked as though there were nearly twenty of them now. The bottom fell out of Tiggy's belly as she remembered how strong they were when she'd encountered them at Haven. She was just about to walk the boarding plank into the shallows, her body trembling all over, when she heard a loud scream from the other side of the cliffs.

The pirates stopped in their tracks.

'What was that?' Marina asked.

'I don't know,' Tiggy replied.

The voice sounded again, only this time, Tiggy could make out words: 'My fin. My fin is stuck, somebody help.'

The pirates turned, dashing from the sloop and towards the voice.

'Well, that was weird,' Miguel said, stroking his stubbled chin as the pirates raced towards the mangroves.

But Tiggy barely heard him. She recognized that voice, and this time it wasn't in her head. *She* was here – the mermaid from her dream.

'That voice,' she said. 'It belonged to the mermaid.'

'She's here?' Marina gasped.

Tiggy nodded.

'So the mermaid . . . ?'

'Must have escaped,' Tiggy said. 'And we have to help her, as she's obviously in grave danger.'

'We help the mermaid or we help your brothers,' Lucia said, positioning herself so she could walk the gangplank into the shallows. 'This is our best chance to get the boys, before the mage returns to his castle.'

Tiggy felt torn. She wished she could help both, but Lucia was right – they had to strike now.

'OK,' she whispered. 'Let's go get our boys.'

The castle emerged from the darkness, a huge stone structure built on several levels so that it followed the upwards sweep of the hill and seemed like part of the island itself. A collection of turrets coiled and scrabbled into the dusk like stone vines, with small bridges suspended between every battlement. Tiggy felt the hairs on the back of her neck stand on end. She had never seen anything like it. It was a castle grown from nightmares and magic, not stone and toil.

Tiggy and Marina ducked behind a lip of rock, the crew beside them.

Lucia exhaled slowly. 'OK, so we need to get in and out as quickly as possible. Rescue the boys and grab all the treasure we can carry, right? Any problems with the pirates and Marina here can serenade them off to sleep.'

'Are we going in now or waiting till morning?' Doc asked.

'Yeah,' Cannon yawned. 'All this talking is making me sleepy. We could have a little nap in this nice, soft grass.'

Lucia scowled, clearly disapproving of Cannon's incessant yawning. 'We go get your brothers and the treasure *now*, before the mage and his men return. Hopefully there'll only be a handful of watchmen.'

'Just the brothers?' Miguel asked, concern registering in his voice.

Lucia nodded.

'No way,' Tiggy said. 'We save *all* the boys, before the mage turns them into Sea Golems.'

A combination of sadness and resignation passed across Lucia's face. 'Tiggy, we don't even know where the pirates keep their fleet when we make our escape. This plan is dodgy at best.'

'That's easy,' Tiggy said. 'Diego and Felipe will know. They arrived on the ships after all.'

'All the same . . .' Lucia began to object.

'We save *all* the boys,' Tiggy repeated, her fists clenched with stubbornness.

'Why don't we get inside and assess the situation then,' Marina offered helpfully.

'I say we storm the gate,' Cannon said, her face dancing with exhilaration. 'Guns blazing, knives drawn, we'll free the boys and find the treasure.'

'That's a terrible idea,' Lucia snapped. 'You didn't see how many pirates raided Haven.'

Cannon looked wounded. 'All right, Captain, you know that's a sore point.'

Lucia sighed. 'The fact is, if we just run in there, we'll be captured in an instant. We need to be smart.'

The crew fell into a stony silence as though the word 'smart' scared them.

'We could sneak in,' Marina offered. 'Maybe climb over the walls, try not to wake anyone.'

'What you need is someone who's good at climbing,' Spider said, wiggling his eyebrows and punching his chest. 'Someone with a deft foot and a steady hand who can climb in and open the gates from the inside.'

Miguel stared at him in disbelief. 'You spend half your time dangling from ropes, lad. You'll get yourself killed trying to climb them there walls.'

Tiggy thought of her padre, as she so often did when trying to solve a problem. She could almost hear his measured voice, and her chest hurt with missing him. 'Padre always said that the best place to hide things was in plain sight. What if we just marched inside like we belong? The adults can pretend to be the mage's men, then Spider, Marina and I could pretend to be your prisoners. You could say we were trying to sneak out and you're bringing us back again. Marina sings the pirates to sleep, and we escape with all the boys.'

Everyone stared at her.

Tiggy suddenly felt very silly. What made her think she could come up with a plan to infiltrate the castle? She fell into string quartets and hacked off her hair, for goodness sake. Holding her breath, she waited for laughter which never came.

'Tiggy, that's genius,' Lucia said.

'One problem,' Miguel said. 'Two of you are girls.'

Tiggy felt a rush of confidence, fuelled on by the success of her suggestion. 'Baggy clothes, hats pulled low. It's not light yet. They'll never tell.'

'I could always hack off Marina's hair,' Cannon said with a wicked grin.

'No way.' Marina clutched her head defensively.

'I'm sure ponytails will be fine, thank you, Cannon,' Lucia replied. 'The bigger problem is that metal grate I can see in front of the doors. Once we're in and it's lowered behind us, we'll never get out.' She turned to Spider. 'Now's your chance to live up to your name. Wait till we're in, then sneak on to the wall and do whatever you need to do. Just make sure you can raise the grate when the time comes.'

He saluted. 'Aye aye, Captain.'

Lucia looked at the rest of the crew, excitement sizzling in her eyes. 'OK. Help Tiggy and Marina prepare. We need to hurry, as the mage will return soon.'

Doc fastened his bandanna around Marina's head and helped her tuck back her hair, whilst Miguel helped Tiggy into his scratchy, loose shirt. Marina then hid her sealskin beneath some rocks and tucked her winkle shell necklace beneath her top.

'How do we look?' Tiggy asked, dropping her voice as low as she could.

'Best not speak if you can help it,' Miguel replied, looking rather chilly in his rum-stained vest.

'Now it's your turn,' Tiggy told them.

The crew stared at her with blank faces.

'You don't look nearly rough enough to be in the mage's crew,' she explained gently.

'Hey!' Cannon exclaimed, positioning her leather weapons belt. 'We're as rough as any pirate.'

'Tiggy's right,' Lucia replied. 'We look like we're going for tea with the Queen.'

'I wouldn't go that far,' Tiggy whispered to a smirking Marina.

The crew then began ruffling themselves up, ripping their clothes and rubbing dirt into their faces. By the time they'd finished, they just looked like slightly more unkempt versions of their previous selves. Tiggy remembered the terrifying pirates who had stolen Diego and Felipe, who had ransacked the port and marched out of the squid's mouth. They had been riddled with scars, filled with venom, wrapped in muscles and weapons. She sighed. The crew before her looked more like a band of beggars, and yet she found her heart overflowing with affection.

She took a deep breath. 'Before we do this, I just want to say that I know you didn't agree to this. You only agreed to take us to the boys, not rescue them. You don't have to risk your lives if—' Her voice broke.

Miguel folded her into a huge embrace. 'Come here, Señorita Tiggy.' His vest smelt of mouldy cheese and whisky, yet she found it strangely comforting.

'Antigua de Fortune,' Lucia said firmly. 'Before we met you and Marina, we were just a bunch of ex-pirates who scrounged a living off the ocean, catching fish and shipping goods. Nobody respected us, we were . . . a bit of a joke.'

'Who's been laughin' at me?' Cannon said, pulling a dagger from her weapons belt. 'If I find 'em, I'll—'

'It's true,' Miguel said, cutting across his friend. 'Cannon hasn't fired a cannon in years, Doc doesn't know a bicep from a femur and Spider would make the worst spider ever. And me . . . well, if that stern ever gets fixed, it'll be a miracle.'

'What's a fee-moo?' Doc whispered to Spider.

Lucia placed her hands on Tiggy and Marina's shoulders. 'You girls have awakened our spirits, shown us things we didn't think possible. This trip ain't about the treasure any more, is it, gang?'

The crew shook their heads.

'We was terrible pirates anyway,' Miguel whispered to Tiggy. 'Why d'ya think we retired?'

Without another word, the crew formed a circle and placed their hands into the middle so that, from above, they resembled the spoked wheel of a cart. Lucia gestured with her head for Tiggy and Marina to do the same.

'It feels like we need a catchphrase or something,' Spider said, once the wheel was complete.

'Go Resolute,' Marina offered.

'Fire in the hole,' Cannon said.

Doc shook his head and looked deep in thought. 'Keep your wounds clean,' he finally said.

Lucia sighed. 'OK, it needs work. Let's just settle

on a quiet *Yo ho ho*.'

'*Yo ho ho*,' came the collective whisper.

And with that, they began to walk towards the snarling teeth of the metal grate.

CHAPTER 28

Clara was so close to the open waves that she could feel the spray on her skin, taste the fresh bite of freedom in the air. But she could see that Felipe's friends were not yet clear of the pirates. And she owed it to the girl to let her find her brother.

Felipe gestured to the approaching pirates. 'They're getting close.'

He was right. Clara could make out their faces now: a selection of oversized, gnarly features, warmed with grog blossom yet hardened with years of hate. Her stomach turned as she recalled her first capture – the grip of their cruel hands and the smirks of their cruel mouths. She watched Antigua reach the peak of the cliffs and disappear into the darkness with her friends. She turned her attention back to the pirates, and noticed with a flash of panic that one of the group was the mage himself. She would recognize those arrogant features anywhere.

Instinctively, she gripped Felipe's hand. 'OK, we have to go. Climb aboard.'

Felipe clambered on to her back and she pushed through the final stretch of the mangrove, the open waters only a few tail-beats away. She was so close, yet she couldn't help glance behind her. Terror transformed her flesh into something cold and rigid, for the mage had reached the base of the cliff and was carving what looked like a turquoise snake into the air. It hovered for a second, glowing luminescent in the dark, then transformed into a blue mist as he shoved his hands towards them.

Carried on the breeze, she heard the word, *Captourer*.

'Quickly,' Felipe called.

Clara flicked her tail as hard as she could, but she found she could no longer move. Pressure closed around her body so that she felt gripped by a monstrous hand. She looked down, dread curdling in her throat, and saw several large snakes coiled around her limbs and body. She gasped, wriggling with all her might while Felipe tried to pull them free.

'The roots,' Felipe yelled. 'The roots of the trees have come to life.'

Clara saw immediately that Felipe was right; she was held fast, not by serpents, but by the roots of the surrounding trees.

'Swim,' Clara shouted to Felipe.

He shook his head. 'I'm not leaving you.'

She watched in horror as the pirates rushed towards them, jumping between the trunks and wading through the narrow streams. They carried a series of grid-like nets and pointed sticks. Clara's vision was spotted with panic, but she could still make out the mage standing on the bay and smiling, the underside of his chin illuminated by the faint glow of his palms.

He held her gaze, and then, with one single motion, swiped his hand through the air so that the roots finally released her into the pirates' nets.

CHAPTER 29

Lucia clanged the butt of her sword against the metal grate. 'Ahoy there, me hearties. Open up, I got me some fresh cargo.'

Tiggy marvelled at how powerful Lucia sounded, how her usual voice vanished beneath a strong pirate drawl. No wonder she was Captain. Tiggy's legs were so weak she was struggling to stand up straight, and she could tell that the rest of the crew were quaking too.

A pink-faced pirate poked his head over the wall above. His hair was so blond it glowed brighter than the moon behind him. 'What d'ya want?'

Lucia cleared her throat. 'We was out by the cliffs and found us some boys trying to escape.'

Moon-hair looked down at Tiggy and Marina. Tiggy purposefully lowered her head so the pirate would not see the nerves which danced across her face.

'Does the boss know?' Moon-hair's voice splintered with panic.

Lucia smiled a cool smile. 'No, but I can tell him if you want?'

'Er . . . best not. If the boss finds out we let some of the boys escape . . .' Moon-hair drew his finger across his neck in a swift motion whilst making a hissing noise which mimicked that of spurting blood.

'No problem,' Lucia called back.

The grate rose up, creaking and groaning beneath its own weight, until it hung above them like a row of knives. Tiggy shivered as Lucia and Doc shoved her beneath it. She sensed Marina beside her, ushered on by Cannon and Miguel. The wooden doors before them then opened, but a pair of pirates blocked their way. One of them had a huge scar across his neck, which gave the impression that his head had been chopped off, only to be badly sewn back on again at a slightly different angle; the other wore a python around his neck like a scarf. The creature blinked lazily at Tiggy, licking the air with its forked tongue.

The Scar stepped towards Tiggy. 'Well, well, well. What have we got here? Escapees?' He raised a fist as if to strike Tiggy's cheek, but Lucia caught it mid-air. 'No need for that,' she said. 'I gave him a good hiding when I found him, the little blighter.'

The Scar laughed, spittle flying from his mouth. 'Pleased to hear it.' He stared at Lucia for a moment. ''Ere, why don't I recognize you?' He turned to his comrade. 'Python, have you seen this lot before?'

Both pirate and python shook their heads, so that Tiggy was unsure which beast was responding to their name.

Lucia shrugged. 'That'll be the grog-rot, your brains are clearly addled.'

For a moment, Tiggy wasn't sure how the pirates would react. Their expressions froze, caught halfway between offence and surprise. Then, much to her relief, they threw back their heads and roared with laughter. Even the snake seemed to smile. 'That'll be it,' the Scar said, gesturing for them to pass through the wooden gates. 'We've got grog-rot, ain't that right, Python?'

Man and snake nodded.

Above the clank of her heart, Tiggy heard the soft thump from above. She imagined Spider clonking Moon-hair over the head. A surge of excitement spread through her abdomen – so far, everything was going according to plan.

She entered the courtyard and tried not to gasp. Even in the gloom, she could see it was spectacular. Turrets twisted into the sky and the surrounding walls jutted upwards like slabs of frozen lava. Dotted across the walls were large metal cages, containing what looked like sleeping birds, and beneath them lay an entire army of dozing pirates, clutching their weapons as though they were teddy bears. Tiggy suppressed a gag as the stench of sweat and old rum invaded her nostrils. She glanced around, anxiety kicking her in the guts . . . the boys weren't there. She tried to control her breathing. They needed to find them, and quickly, before the mage returned.

Lucia had obviously come to the same conclusion. 'I'll put these boys with the others if you want,' she said to the Scar.

He shrugged. 'They're in the dungeons. Brute will take you.' The man-mountain appeared, jangling a set of rusted keys at them. 'Brute,' he barked.

Just seeing Brute again and the memory of the raid hit Tiggy square in the chest. She ordered her breathing to remain calm so as not to draw suspicion.

'Why don't I take those,' Lucia asked, reaching for the keys. But Brute whipped them away and wagged a finger at her. 'Brute's,' he said, tucking them into his belt.

Tiggy felt her nails cut into her palms. This wasn't the plan, but perhaps Marina could sing as soon as they reached the boys and then they could grab the keys from a very sleepy Brute. Her skin prickled with anticipation and concern. There were so many things which could go wrong.

The Scar stepped in front of them. 'Hang on,' he said, leaning towards Marina and peering at her necklace with a curious expression. 'What be this? A pretty wee selkie charm? Where d'ya steal this, me laddo?' His fist closed around it.

Panic engulfed Marina's face. She opened her mouth as if to sing, aware this may be her one chance, but the pirate ripped the charm from her body before a single note could leave her lips.

'No!' Tiggy gasped.

The Scar glared at her. 'What's that?'

'I ... I ...' Tiggy stammered.

Miguel clipped her round the head. 'Lad's been chuntering all the way here. I think he's a fool.'

The Scar nodded and fastened the charm around his neck. 'Aye, that'll be right. Too much school and not enough rum, it'd turn the best of us into blithering fools.' He turned to his huge comrade. 'Now, be a good Brute and take 'em to the dungeons.' He glared at the crew. 'Go too, stay on guard till they're safely locked up again.'

Brute led Tiggy, Marina and the crew through a dimly lit archway and down a staircase which was carved into the rock and lit with blazing torches. They spiralled deeper and deeper into the ground until Tiggy began to feel a little light-headed, the air thin and damp. She had expected the temperature to drop, but instead she grew hot and clammy. They were right next to the heart of the volcano. She could sense its power.

With every step, her brain whirred. Surely she and the crew could overpower Brute and grab the keys. He was a beast of a man, and Padre had failed, but now it was six against one. Then they just needed to get Marina's necklace back.

They finally reached the dungeons, a series of barred caves stretching into a darkness like the very guts of the volcano itself. Torches flickered on the walls, throwing angular shadows across the rocks. At least a hundred dirty faces pressed up against the bars, the boys woken by their arrival. The sight of those little fingers curling around the metal poles made Tiggy's heart sting. She looked for Diego and Felipe, but it was too dark to pick them out.

Brute unlocked the barred door of the largest cell and shoved Tiggy and Marina inside. They landed with a bump against the hard, jagged floor. Pain lunged up Tiggy's hip and into her chest. The door clanged shut and Tiggy helped Marina stand, trying desperately not to cry for the sake of her friend.

'I can lock up,' Lucia said, holding out her hand for the key.

Brute shook his head, sending his white hair floating around his face like clouds. He jabbed a finger against his chest and repeated in his gruff, mountain-like voice, 'Brute.'

Tiggy noticed Cannon and Miguel sneak behind Brute, freeing weapons from their belts.

Lucia merely raised an eyebrow. 'And tell me, Brute, when will the boys next be allowed out of the dungeons?'

'Brute,' came the reply.

Lucia smiled. 'OK. Glad we cleared that up.'

Cannon raised a rifle above her head and slammed the butt into Brute's head. She grunted with the effort but, just like when Padre tried, Brute merely rubbed his hair as though an annoying gnat had bitten him. He turned and looked at Cannon, who shoved the rifle behind her back and offered a sheepish grin.

'Brute?' the man said, as if Cannon had tapped him and tried to get his attention.

'I just wanted to say,' Cannon said, searching desperately for words. 'Nice dungeons.'

He grinned. 'Brute,' he said happily.

Now it was Miguel's turn. He lifted a rock from the ground, jumped into the air and let it smash against Brute's head. Tiggy waited for Brute to crumple to the ground, but instead he merely swayed, blinking quickly.

He turned to face Miguel. 'Brute?'

Miguel sighed, massaging his wrist as though he'd sustained the injury. 'Yeah, nice dungeons, Brute. Good job.'

Brute grinned.

The crew looked at Tiggy and Marina and shrugged as if to say, *we tried*. Then they turned and followed Brute back up the staircase.

Before she left, Lucia pushed her face between the bars. 'Don't worry, we'll get that necklace back and get you out of here.' Then she sprinted up the stairs, leaving Tiggy and Marina staring forlornly at the empty space she'd just occupied.

They were locked in a dungeon till morning with no selkie necklace.

This wasn't the plan.

Fear and self-doubt pressed down on Tiggy's shoulders, crushing the air from her lungs and causing her legs to tremble. Quickly, she studied the boys, all staring silently at her. She recognized a few of them: one was the butcher's son, another was the younger brother of one of their maids back home. Yet they looked somehow different. Hungrier, dirtier, as though a part of their souls had already been stolen. And just as she was about to sink into the floor, the hopelessness overcoming her completely, a little voice reached across the cell.

'Tig? Is that really you?'

She turned. There, in the corner, hunched and crying, his striped nightgown marbled with dirt, was Diego. Their eyes met and he let out a little yelp of delight. Tiggy dashed to him and scooped him into her arms. He began to cry even harder, though he wore the biggest smile Tiggy had ever seen. 'Oh, Tig. You came for me,' he managed to say between sobs.

'Shhh,' she whispered, stroking his muddy, tear-drenched face. 'Course I did.'

She pulled Bobo from her shirt and nestled him in Diego's arms. Her little brother sank his face into the teddy's soft fur, sighing slightly. For a tiny moment, Tiggy felt like maybe everything would be OK.

Marina knelt beside them and gave Diego a warm embrace. 'Where's Felipe?' she asked him softly.

'He escaped with the mermaid,' Diego replied.

All of the colour drained from Marina's face. She caught Tiggy's eye and grimaced.

'You never know,' Tiggy said. 'Maybe she freed her fin in time and they swam to get help.'

Marina didn't reply, her face tight with worry.

'Tig, I'm hungry,' Diego said.

'We'll be home soon, promise. Then I'll ask Cook to make us the biggest dinner ever.'

'Bigger than a whale?' he asked, his eyes shining.

Tiggy nodded. 'Bigger than an island.' She snuggled around Diego and pulled Marina close so she joined their huddle. 'All we can do now is wait till the morning light. Lucia will sort it, I know she will. The Bloodmoon isn't until tomorrow night, so we've still got time to get out of here.' She hoped her voice sounded strong, hoped it didn't show the panic which rose in her stomach.

'Will we be back in time for the carnival?' Diego asked.

'Of course, silly guppy,' she said, stroking his hair. And gradually, listening to the sound of the other boys sleeping, the fizz of moisture in the rock and the occasional tap of rodents' claws as they scooted past looking unsuccessfully for food, she drifted into an uneasy sleep.

CHAPTER 30

She was woken by the sound of the cell opening. A blur of boots and hardened faces, and Felipe was tossed inside. He was missing his wooden leg, and hopped for a moment, before steadying himself against the bars.

Marina flung herself around him.

'Marina, how did you get here?' Felipe asked, returning her embrace. Fear quickly chased the joy from his face as he realized his sister was in the lion's den too. His eyes then settled on Tiggy and he offered a wobbly smile. 'We saw you, on board the

Resolute,' he said, whilst Marina helped him towards her. 'What in Kraken's name are you doing here?'

Marina glanced around and lowered her voice. 'We came to save you. Don't worry, we've got friends on the outside.'

'The crew from the *Resolute*?' Felipe asked, unable to hide his disappointment. 'They'll be no match for the mage and his men.'

'We've got a secret weapon,' Tiggy said, nudging Marina gently.

'*Had* a secret weapon,' Marina said sadly. 'It won't work without the necklace.'

'We'll get it back,' Tiggy said. 'I mean, that pirate looked like his head was about to fall off.'

Marina made a noise halfway between a snigger and snuffle. 'I guess.'

'What's happened?' Felipe asked.

'Oh, not a lot,' Tiggy replied, pretending to be cool. 'Only that . . . Marina's a selkie.'

Felipe clapped his sister around the back. 'I *knew* it. Ah, that's brilliant, sis. I wish I could transform into a seal.'

'You're not scared of me?' Marina asked.

Felipe shook his head. 'No way. I know a lot of land folk are funny about magical sea creatures, but

Madre's a selkie, and Clara, that's the mermaid I was with, she's awesome. She's the mermaid who helped save me the day I lost my leg.'

'How do selkies wipe their bums when they're seals?' Diego interrupted. 'Surely their flippers are too short to reach.'

Tiggy and Felipe laughed.

'Diego,' Marina scolded.

Diego shrugged. 'You'll have to let me know, Mari.'

'Was that you then?' Tiggy asked Felipe. 'Down at the cliffs?'

Felipe nodded, the light from the torches causing shadows to flit across his face. 'Yep, me and a mermaid, Clara. We could see the pirates coming, so we tried to create a diversion so you could all escape.'

'Thank you,' Tiggy said.

Felipe sighed. 'Clara was pretty cut up about being captured again, but she said she owed you. She told the mage the prophecy of the Bloodmoon, you see.'

Tiggy nodded. 'Your madre told us about it, but she didn't know the actual words.'

'Only the merfolk know that,' Felipe said. 'Though Clara did tell me.' He paused.

'Well . . .' Marina prompted.

He sighed. 'I can't remember it word for word.'

'For goodness sake, Felipe,' Marina said. 'What *can* you remember?'

'Well, it said that the curse will reawaken when a boy of Haven falls at the hand of the mage beneath the Bloodmoon. So there's going to be a sacrifice tomorrow night.'

Tiggy gasped. 'That's awful. So the mage kills one of you, and the rest of you turn into Sea Golems?'

Felipe broke eye contact, ashamed at the terror which flashed in his eyes. 'I'm afraid so.'

'Does the mage know which boy?' Marina asked.

'No,' Felipe replied. 'That's why the mage has Clara, to force her to identify the right boy.'

'So it could be any of you?' Tiggy asked, her eyes anxiously clicking to Diego.

Felipe scrunched up his nose, trying to remember the exact words. 'She said something about the child being born of a wave. That's it . . . a child of Haven, born of a wave.'

Tiggy stared at Felipe, sympathy flooding her system. 'Oh, Felipe,' she whispered.

Marina looked as though she'd been punched in the gut. 'Born of a wave . . . it's what the selkies call their children, *born of a wave*,' she stammered. 'It's *you*, Felipe. *You're* the boy from the prophecy.'

CHAPTER 31

The next morning, Tiggy and the rest of the prisoners were awoken by the mage's men and dragged up the long, winding staircase which linked the dungeons to the outside world. Tiggy's muscles ached with every step, her head rang with fatigue, but she had only one thing on her mind as she stepped into the sunny courtyard: she must somehow get the selkie charm back to Marina so they could escape.

The pirates ushered the crowd of scared children towards the back wall of the battlements. Tiggy noticed how the boys were clinging to each other, both for comfort and in a bid to remain standing in spite of dehydration and hunger. Clutching Diego's hand, she forced out a reassuring smile and pretended she wasn't afraid, when really every fibre of her being stung with fear. She caught Felipe's eye. Last night he had promised them again and again that Clara would not reveal him as the boy from the prophecy, yet his drawn face and clenched jaw suggested his confidence was waning.

Squinting against the morning sun, Tiggy took in her surroundings. They were encased by steep volcanic walls and angry-looking pirates, and in spite of the expanse of blue above, she felt like one of the many gulls trapped in the large cages which swung from barricades. The birds followed her with their beady eyes, ruffling their feathers and squawking like warning bells. She hated this place. Desperately, she searched the pirates for Lucia and the rest of the crew, concerned for their safety and keen to see if they'd retrieved Marina's necklace.

But her eyes found somebody else.

Chained to a boulder, right in the centre of the courtyard, was the mermaid from her dreams. The poor creature wasn't in salt water, not even a shallow pool. Everyone knew that mermaids couldn't last long outside the ocean; her scales already looked cracked and sore.

The mage stepped in front of the crowd of prisoners. 'So, here we are again.' He pointed first at Clara, and then Felipe. 'Well, you have fishface and this silly boy to blame.' He laughed and threw Felipe's wooden leg on the ground.

A bolt of anger flashed through Tiggy. How dare this evil mage mock her friend so. She clenched her fists and turned her attention to the crew of the *Resolute*. She saw them, all except Spider, blending into the pirates around the back of the boulder. Lucia held her gaze for a moment, and then shook her head very slowly. Tiggy knew what she meant immediately: she'd been unable to retrieve the selkie necklace. Disheartened, Tiggy twisted her neck around and located the Scar, not far from them at the back of the courtyard. Around his neck, glinting in the sun, hung Marina's charm.

She tugged at Marina's hand. 'Back there,' she whispered. 'I can see your necklace.' Ever so slowly, she and her friends began edging back, all the while watching the mage as he switched his attention from the boys back to Clara.

'Well, salt-drinker,' he said, towering over the mermaid. 'You have no tank this time. Let's see how long you last beneath the rays of the sun.'

Clara recoiled slightly, a strange sensation passing over her. It was as though her skin was shrinking in the absence of sea. She tried to swallow, tried to blink, but there was no moisture left in her body. She felt that at any moment she would vanish in a cloud of sand and settle on the concrete floor, leaving nothing but a golden swirl of beach upon the grey.

'Please,' Felipe cried. 'She won't even last the day. You have to find her another tank.'

The pirates jeered and the gulls screeched, yet the mage didn't even acknowledge Felipe had spoken. Instead, he leant into the mermaid and gripped her chin. 'Tell me, sea beast, which of these boys is the boy from the prophecy.'

Through her pain, Clara noticed the vial around his neck. Up close, she could see that it was filled with a dark, viscous liquid . . . oil perhaps.

The mage noticed her line of sight and chuckled. 'I'll tell you what this is in good time. But first, tell me – *which boy is the boy from the prophecy?*'

She glared into the mage's eyes. 'I will never tell you.'

'Fine, have it your way.' He released Clara's face, allowing her to slump backwards. 'You know these birds haven't been fed in a *very* long time.' A menacing smile hung on his lips. 'And what they crave more than anything else is sea beast.' Turquoise light sizzled between his hands and the gulls in the cages roared like a pack of hungry wolves. Slowly, as if enjoying the drama, the mage proceeded to slice into the air the shape of a key. But instead of thrusting his hands towards Clara as she had expected, he turned and shot his hands upwards, towards the battlements of the castle.

The word, *Mortari*, escaped from his lips.

A series of clicks echoed around the castle walls, followed by the squeak of metal doors swinging open. The birds paused, noticing their sudden escape route, then all at once launched themselves towards the mermaid, talons out and beaks ajar.

'No!' Tiggy gasped.

Clara began to scream as the swarm of gulls nipped at her skin and her scales. She flapped her hands above her head, beat her purple tail, but it was no use – there were simply too many birds to knock away. The pain engulfed her . . . *became her* . . . until she was sure she would simply disappear, picked to pieces by the vicious gulls.

Tiggy watched on, desperate to help, desperate to rush forwards and clobber those feathered demons with all her might, but she knew the best way to help was to get Marina's necklace, and so she fought her natural instinct and focused on creeping towards the Scar, tugging Diego along beside her.

The mage waved his hand and the gulls lifted like an angry veil, leaving a very sorry-looking Clara lying on the ground, cuts and scrapes criss-crossing her body and fins. The birds hovered only yards above her head – a seething cloud of bloodied beaks and claws. She slumped against her boulder, exhausted and shredded with pain.

'Now will you tell me?' the mage asked. 'The birds have only just started, after all.'

It would be so easy to tell him what he wanted to know. So easy to save herself. Yet a strange, determined look set into Clara's features. 'I will not tell you, mage. Not this time.'

Clara awaited another onslaught of feathers, talons and hurt. But it never came. Instead, the mage knelt before her and reached behind his neck, unfastening the chain which held the vial to his throat. The tiny bottle swung from his hand, glinting in the morning sun. The dark liquid sloshed inside like an angry sea.

'Do you know what this is, salt-drinker?'

Clara shook her head.

The mage removed the cork from the top of the vial and tipped a tiny drop of the dark liquid on to his tongue. He closed his eyes and sighed as though savouring the taste. Then, carefully, almost lovingly, he repositioned the cork and leant into Clara. He was so close, she could feel his breath against the scales on her cheeks, so close she could see something odd happening to his face: the lines around his eyes were fading, his lips grew slightly plumper and his skin seemed to tighten around his cheekbones and chin. The mage was growing younger before her very eyes. She blinked quickly, trying to clear her head. Surely it was just the dehydration and torture playing tricks on her.

The mage watched her and smiled, his teeth whiter. 'Have you ever wondered who I am? After all, a mage as powerful as myself has not existed since the Pirate King all those years ago.'

Clara nodded, even though it hurt her skin to move, fractures seeming to form at her every joint.

'And have you ever wondered how I command the ocean like the Pirate King? How I *magnify* its magic between my hands, just like he did?'

Again, Clara forced out a nod. She had wondered this non-stop since meeting the wicked man.

The mage pressed his lips against her ear and whispered. 'I drink the blood of merfolk, Clara.' He held the vial up so she could see. 'That's right. I drink the blood of your people. At first, after they tried to murder me all those years ago, I could barely move. I sank to the ocean floor, and there I lay, a shadow of my former self, feeding on algae and the corpses of fallen fish. As the years passed, I gathered strength and I was able to feast on lobsters, even the odd dolphin and shark. And eventually, I began to feed on magical creatures themselves. The selkies and the merfolk. Your blood built me up – it restored my youth and my power.'

'I . . . I don't understand,' she whispered.

'I'm able to command the ocean like the Pirate King, because I *am* the Pirate King. They didn't kill me; they merely slowed me down. And now I have risen, and I want my Golems back.'

'Sweet Kraken,' she murmured, her voice rasping in her throat.

'And this vial contains the blood of someone very special indeed.' He paused, before whispering in a dangerous, low voice, '*Your mother.*'

CHAPTER 32

Clara drew back. A pain far worse than any gull could inflict grew inside her stomach, a pain which ate her from the inside and from which she could never escape. Her mother. Lost when she was only a child, Clara still recalled the warmth of her smile, the gentle lilt of her voice and the soft press of skin as she rocked her to sleep.

Clara had never known how she had died; her padre had refused to tell her. Well, now she knew – this *monster* had killed her. With her last remaining strength, Clara raised her fists, only to remember she was still shackled to the blasted boulder.

The Pirate King kept his voice a soft hiss so only she could hear. 'I recognized you as soon as I saw you, for you are the image of her. Same purple scales, same glint of mischief in your eyes.' He chuckled.

Clara shook her head, disbelief and disgust pooling in her stomach. 'You're a monster.'

'Perhaps. Better a monster who cheats death than a man who submits to the grave.' He touched the scales on Clara's cheek, causing her to shiver. 'Anyway, she never told me the prophecy, but I was able to draw many vials of blood from your mother's veins before she died. Alas, I'm down to my last one.' He made a noise somewhere between a laugh and a sigh. 'Merfolk are incredibly hard to capture but, lucky for me, you swam too close to my ship that day. Were you curious, Clara? Or were you drawn to me? Drawn to the scent of your mother's blood?'

Clara faltered. She couldn't recall why she'd swum so close to the ship that day, why she'd ignored the warnings of her loved ones. Was she merely curious, or had something stronger lured her there?

The mage continued. 'How fortunate that so close to the Bloodmoon I not only discovered the prophecy, but also a new supply of mermaid blood.'

He pinched the underbelly of her upper arm. 'I wonder how many vials I'll get from you.'

Her anger evaporated, giving way to a tidal wave of fear. She opened her mouth to object, but only a small wail of distress emerged.

"There is a way out of this, of course,' he continued, refastening the vial around his neck. 'You show me the boy from the prophecy, and I will set you free, once I've extracted what I need, naturally.'

Clara gazed from the vial to the Pirate King's eyes. They were far harder, far cooler, than the glass which contained her mother's blood. She simply couldn't let him reawaken the curse and reignite his reign of terror, no matter what the cost. 'I will tell you *nothing*,' she hissed, her voice a dry croak.

The Pirate King stood, raising his voice. 'I didn't want to do this, it requires so much energy, uses up so much of my fuel, but seeing as I have a fresh supply.' He tipped the remainder of the vial down his neck and, slowly, let his head fall backwards; his eyeballs rolled back into their sockets so only the whites remained. The turquoise light seemed to be coming from inside him now, filling his mouth and his eyes.

Clara felt something stir inside. A deep force

which shook every fibre of her being and left her terrified, hollow and distraught all at once. The Pirate King looked down at the mermaid, his face glowing bright turquoise, and when he finally spoke, his voice sounded different . . . terrifying and magical . . . whale song, crashing waves and low rumbling thunder combined into one. 'Point to the one who will usher in my reign.'

Clara struggled to breathe, her ribs seeming to crush the air from her lungs, her gills sucking frantically at water which would never arrive. The feeling of emptiness and doom vanished, replaced only by a soul-sucking blankness. Every memory wiped, every thought and emotion blotted out in a cloud of nothingness. She didn't even know her name. The determined expression was ripped from her face as if it were merely a mask. Her head fell backwards and her eyes became all white, just like the Pirate King's had done only moments ago. The turquoise light pushed its way from her mouth and her eyes, bright spindly rays, like terrifying fingers.

Everyone inside the courtyard froze, too afraid to move, too afraid to even breathe.

Everyone except Tiggy. And even though her heart thrummed with fear, even though she could barely tear her eyes from Clara's transformation, she was only a few small steps away from Marina's necklace – and she *had* to reach it before Clara identified Felipe.

But before she could grab the charm from the Scar's neck, she heard Clara's voice, loud and clear as it rang across the courtyard. 'The child who must fall beneath the Bloodmoon stands before you, my Lord.'

The crowd parted, and Tiggy saw that the mermaid was pointing straight at them.

The Pirate King allowed his gaze to settle on Felipe. 'So it *was* you after all,' he whispered, his voice low.

Everything happened at once. Clara collapsed as the light left her mouth in a puff of blue mist, the pirates rushed towards Felipe, blades drawn, and Tiggy grabbed the necklace from the throat of the Scar and thrust it into her best friend's hands.

Immediately the necklace began to fill with turquoise light, glowing inside Marina's palms just as it had back at the sloop. Not wasting a second, Marina threw back her head, opened her mouth and released the purest note Tiggy had ever heard. It soared high above the castle walls, swooping and diving into a stunning melody which echoed around the volcanic walls and sated the cracked stone of the courtyard floor.

One by one, the pirates swayed on the spot before falling to their knees and slumping to the floor. Eventually the mage himself began to crumble, still drained from his possession of Clara. Miguel and Lucia hurled themselves at him, ropes ready.

Diego took the opportunity to fetch Felipe his wooden leg.

'Marina, that is so cool,' Felipe called as he fastened his leg back into position.

She continued to sing, the melody weaving higher and higher, holding the pirates fast in their enchanted sleep. Hundreds of boys raced towards the wooden gates, battering at them with their fists.

Tiggy dashed towards the mermaid, skidding the final stretch on her knees. 'Are you OK?'

Clara raised her bloodshot eyes towards her. 'Antigua de Fortune. We meet at last.'

Tiggy noticed how cracked her skin looked, how dull her scales were, as though her tail had been wrapped in paper. 'We've got to get you to salt water,' Tiggy said, pulling on the chains. But they were thick, stubborn and simply refused to budge.

'Hang on.' Clara pressed her fingers together,

summoning the magic from within, but nothing happened – not even a flicker. She sighed with frustration. 'My magic . . . it doesn't work so well out of water, especially not when I'm weak.' She looked at Tiggy, sadness enveloping her features. 'At least I helped you find your brother, Tiggy.'

Tiggy squeezed Clara's hand. 'No, I won't let you die here. There must be a way of breaking these chains.' Tiggy felt something sizzle in her fingertips, similar to the sensation she'd felt when she'd touched Gabriella back on the *Resolute*. She retracted her hand as though burnt. Then, without thought, she tried it again, resting her palm in Clara's. Something crackled, the sound of water hitting hot coals. Tiggy looked down to see a fizz of turquoise dancing across her and Clara's hands.

Clara looked at her with surprise. 'How did you do that?'

Tiggy snatched her hand away again. 'I . . . I didn't do anything. It must have been you.'

Clara smiled, revealing a set of sharpened teeth. 'That wasn't me, Antigua. That was *us*. Here, try again, but this time don't pull away.'

And as Tiggy obeyed, a strange sensation passed through her palm: a buzz of static, a whir of something cool and pleasant. Her nostrils filled with scents of the ocean and her skin prickled as though she'd been freshly dipped in the sea.

'You feel it?' Clara asked.

Tiggy nodded, her jaw slack and her chest heaving. 'What . . . what is it?'

Clara grinned. 'It is the magic of the ocean, the sorcery of the waves. It must run inside you, Antigua de Fortune: that is how I can link with you. You're a mage.'

CHAPTER 33

A laugh of disbelief burst from Tiggy's lips. 'I'm not a mage, I mean, I would know if I was a mage, surely.'

'I bet you never ventured into the sea before now, did you?'

Tiggy shook her head. 'I've never been allowed. I learnt to swim in freshwater rivers.'

Clara shrugged. 'Well, then how would you know? Our magic is weak without the ocean. Come. Leave your hands on mine, then I may be able to draw from both sources.' She nodded towards her upturned palms. 'Hurry, for your selkie friend is tiring, I believe.'

Tiggy didn't need to look at her friend to know that the mermaid was right. Marina's voice was starting to waver, the strength dwindling and the notes growing slightly discordant. Tiggy took a deep breath and wove her fingers through the mermaid's, so tight it was difficult to tell where one girl began and the other ended. A tingle of something cool and lovely grew beneath Tiggy's palms, only this time stronger. It spread from her hands, right up her arms, until her entire body was filled with the lapping of waves and the shafts of sunshine in deep waters.

Tiggy watched in awe as a flash of blue light spread beneath their fingertips and the chain cracked as though an invisible pick had struck it.

Clara looked at Tiggy with urgency. 'We mustn't let the Pirate King know about your magic.'

'What do you mean, the Pirate King?' Tiggy asked, fear weighing down her heart.

'The mage. He told me, whispered it so that only I could hear. He isn't a relative of the Pirate King . . . he *is* the Pirate King. He was never killed, just injured, and he built himself back up again by drinking the blood of selkies and mermaids.'

Tiggy gasped. 'Actually *drinking* the blood of magical creatures. But that's horrific.'

'It is. But now we know who the child from the prophecy is, we can stop the curse from awakening. We can stop his reign of terror before it really starts.' Her face filled with concern. 'Just now, the Pirate King seemed to possess me and everything went blank. Did I point to the child?'

Tiggy nodded sadly. 'Yes. You pointed to Felipe. He's of selkie blood, so it makes sense . . . you know, born of a wave. He's the boy from the prophecy.'

Clara released a frustrated sigh. 'Male dominance is still alive and well on land, I see.'

'What do you mean?'

'To automatically ignore females like that, Antigua, it's positively archaic. I didn't say it was a *boy* – I said it was a *child*.'

The realization filled Tiggy with horror.

Gabriella had two children after all.

'Marina!' Tiggy gasped, clutching her stomach as if the revelation had punched her. 'She was standing with me next to Felipe when you pointed at us.'

Of course it was Marina. Selkie blood and born of a wave. How could she have been so stupid? Tears of anger filled her eyes. Nobody she loved was safe from the Pirate King. Padre was dead. Diego and Felipe would become Golems. And now her best friend might die, sacrificed beneath the Bloodmoon.

Clara shook her head. 'No, Antigua de Fortune. There is another girl of Haven who has ocean magic in her blood, another girl who is born of a wave.' She gestured to the broken chains which surrounded her. 'I always suspected, but I didn't truly know until just now.'

Tiggy shook her head, confusion clouding her thoughts. 'I . . . I . . . don't understand.'

Clara sighed, then pointed a finger at Tiggy's chest. 'You!'

'Me,' she squeaked. Her ribcage tightened and her stomach felt ready to heave. 'It can't be me. There must be some mistake.'

Clara shook her head. 'I'm afraid not. It is you, sorceress of the sea. *You* are the child from the prophecy.'

CHAPTER 34

Tiggy opened her mouth to object when a new, more immediate threat raised its head. She looked at Clara, fear reflected in the mermaid's eyes.

It was the singing.

It had stopped.

Marina was slumped forwards on her knees and heaving in great ragged breaths, all of her strength clearly stolen by the melody. Tiggy was about to run to her when the sound of the wooden doors finally caving in ricocheted around the courtyard.

'Spider,' Lucia yelled. 'Raise the grate.'

Tiggy turned to see the grate lifting and a look of joy infecting every single face of the Haven boys.

Lucia raised her sword. 'To the galleons,' she yelled.

The boys thundered from the castle like a herd of startled cows – screaming, whooping and kicking up the dust. From the chaos, Miguel appeared; he lugged Clara over his shoulder, grunting as her tail flopped against the ground.

'Come on, Seňorita Tiggy,' he said. 'We have to go.'

'Diego, Felipe?' she gasped.

'Don't worry, they're with the crew. Quickly, before the pirates wake up.'

Tiggy glanced at the pirates, still dozing on the floor; a few eyelids were beginning to flicker, a few mouths beginning to yawn. 'The mage?' Fear lanced clean through her chest.

'We tied him up best we could,' Miguel replied. 'But the ropes won't hold long – he's starting to come round. Come on.'

Tiggy took the weight of Clara's tail and they staggered towards the gates as quickly as they could.

'Spider,' Miguel yelled. 'Lower the grate.'

She heard the grate clang shut behind them and Spider caught them up, a massive scowl plastered across his face. 'My best climbing *ever*, and none of you saw.'

The boys were running up the volcano, towards the entrance to the underground caves and the Pirate King's fleet, a horde of dirty clothes, scraped knees and excited cries. As she followed, Tiggy automatically scanned the crowd for Felipe or Diego, but they were nowhere to be seen. Just then, she felt something tug on her dungarees, and when she looked down, Diego was beside her. 'I saw you help the mermaid,' he said, his voice jolting from the effort of running up hill. 'Did you use magic?'

Tiggy nodded; the memory of the blue light planted a strange mixture of excitement and trepidation in her stomach. 'I think I did.'

Miguel laughed. 'I always knew you was special, Señorita Tiggy.'

'Madre is going to freak out,' Diego said.

'She's not the only one,' Tiggy replied. 'I mean, a few days ago I'd never even met a sorcerer, now I am one.' She glanced at her hands, still clasped around Clara's tail, afraid they may burst into turquoise flames on their own accord.

'Does this mean you can fight the evil mage?' Diego punched the air. 'Take that, you nasty piece of turtle poo.'

'No way,' she said. 'We escape. Once the Blood-moon passes you'll all be safe.' She ignored her brother's complaints that they might cancel the Carnival, and watched as the boys began vanishing beneath a stone arch sunk into the side of the volcano.

'They're going inside the volcano?' Tiggy asked.

'There's a load of caves that lead out to the sea,' Diego told her. 'It's where they keep the ships.'

An explosion reverberated from behind and they turned to see a bolt of turquoise lightning flash within the courtyard of the castle.

'The mage,' Miguel said. 'He must have blasted the grate. We don't have much time.'

Panic spread through Tiggy's body, but she managed to keep hold of the mermaid's dry, heavy tail and enter the monstrous cave. The light levels dipped and the echoes of the excited boys mixed with the sound of lapping water. The cavern held an entire fleet of ships, bobbing gently in a giant pool, and more treasure than she could comprehend.

'To the largest galleon,' Lucia boomed. 'And bring treasure!'

The boys and crew rumbled down the stone paths towards the ship, grabbing handfuls of treasure as they passed. The gangplanks still remained in position from when Clara's tank had been lugged across; the wooden bridge strained beneath the weight of the swarm.

As Tiggy, Miguel and Diego neared the galleon, Clara raised a sleepy head. 'Release me, please,' she whispered.

Miguel peered over the ledge into the shallows below. 'It's one heck of a drop. You sure you don't want to wait till we're in open waters.'

'I won't last that long,' she replied.

Tiggy had so many questions to ask the mermaid – about the blue magic which crackled beneath their fingertips, about the prophecy and the Pirate King – but she noticed that the scales around Clara's face had turned completely grey and any remaining purple was beginning to leach from her tail. There was no time for questions. 'She's going to die if we don't release her now,' she said.

Miguel nodded and, without any ceremony, they gently dropped her over the ledge. She fell straight down, sandwiched between the rock face and the side of the galleon yet missing both, and hit the water with a loud splash. Tiggy held her breath, not knowing whether or not the mermaid was safe. Then the violet tail broke the surface, and Tiggy released a sigh of relief as Clara vanished in a mass of bubbles.

Grateful for the distraction, Tiggy took a second to admire the galleon. It was just like the kind Padre had sailed; indeed, it had probably been stolen from the Navy. It made the *Resolute* look like a rowing boat. It boasted four large masts, several decks and was covered in ornate carvings which were painted reds and golds. At the front of the ship was the largest beakhead Tiggy had ever seen, a cradle of wood located just below the bowsprit, sporting images of skulls and water snakes. The pirates had obviously redecorated.

Spider gawped beside her. 'Just look at all those crow's-nests. It's like I've died and gone to heaven.'

Poor Miguel had a different take, his brow knotted and his hands clutching his cheeks. 'A stern this size is gonna need a lot more fixing.'

Felipe and Cannon already stood on deck, beckoning frantically from amidst the mound of looted treasure. 'Come on, you dozy blighters,' Cannon said. 'Hop aboard.'

'Some cheek, calling us dozy,' Spider grumbled as they raced across the planks.

Tiggy landed on the ship's deck with a reassuring thud. The wood felt sturdy and, for the first time in days, she felt safe. Holding Diego to her body, she whispered, 'We're nearly there.'

Lucia grabbed the rigging and swung on to the bowsprit, claiming the ship as her own. With a loud, clear voice, she addressed the boys. 'OK, lads. The little ones, get to cabin quarters. Eat and drink whatever you find. The older ones, stay on board and grab an oar. We haven't got long.' She pointed her sword at Cannon. 'And Cannon. Load the big guns. We need to sink the rest of the fleet so the blighters can't follow us.'

Cannon wiped a tear of joy from her eye. 'Oh, Captain . . . thank you.'

Tiggy stood at the helm with her little brother, Marina and Felipe; the four friends linked arms so they became a single unit, and gazed around the monstrous cave as the ship lurched forwards and began to move away from the mountains of treasure and the winding, stone paths. There must have been at least ten other boats, all tethered and bobbing in the shallow water. Tiggy even recognized a few of them from the raid on Haven.

'Where's Clara?' Felipe asked.

'We released her into the water,' Tiggy replied.

A look of sadness flitted across his face. 'And she just left? Without saying goodbye or anything?'

Tiggy nodded. 'She was very ill. That awful mage nearly killed her.'

'How did you free her from her chains?' Marina asked.

'There will be plenty of time to explain,' she replied.

'She used magic,' Diego replied.

Marina's eyes widened – a mixture of surprise and also relief that she wasn't the only one to possess magic. 'What a pair we make, eh?' She gestured to the cloak tucked beneath her arm. She must have retrieved it as they fled the castle. 'One day I'll muster up the courage to wear this.'

The opening to a large tunnel emerged. It was big enough for the ship and was certainly the route back to the ocean. Tiggy could sense the pull of the waves, the call of the open sky for ever tinged with sea spray.

As they neared the tunnel, the galleon turned ninety degrees so its side faced the remaining fleet. Tiggy heard the click of the cannons standing to attention, the thunder of balls loading and the fizz of flames. Could Cannon really do this without falling asleep?

BOOM! The first blast was loudest, shaking the entire cave and causing the surface of the water to tighten then relax. *Boom, boom, boom.* The blast of the cannons filled their ears like a thunderous drum, sending vibrations up their legs and into their chests. The fleet before them exploded, great chunks of wood sailing into the air, and Tiggy remembered with a stab of pain Padre's ship sinking beneath the onslaught of cannons. She turned away, the memory too great to bear.

The sound of the cannons stopped, replaced only by the sound of Cannon's whoops from the deck below. And, slowly, the great galleon turned back on course and headed through the tunnel towards the sea.

CHAPTER 35

The cool of the ocean embraced Clara's body, rejuvenating her cracked scales, soothing her lacerated skin and calming her heart as it flailed inside her chest. She pushed the memory of her darling mother aside, refusing to think about the vial of dark liquid and the mage's cruel, mocking face. She had a job to do.

The Bloodmoon was tonight and she didn't have long.

She slipped beneath the hull of the great galleon, and within moments had hurtled down the tunnels and broken into the open sea, a smile of pure joy dancing on her face. Even at this speed, it would take hours to reach the Fortune Isles, but there was no other option. She closed her eyes, gauged the direction of the currents against her skin and used the familiar shape of the coral floor to plot her route to Tiggy's homeland.

She would make this right.

CHAPTER 36

The underpass delivered the galleon into the hands of the ocean like a gift. Tiggy cherished the sea breeze against her face, the tang of fish and salt against her lips, and the blue-green cloth of water stretching before her. But most of all, she cherished the shape of her little brother, pressed against her hip as he nuzzled Bobo to his cheek.

She'd done it. With the help of her friends, and a mermaid, she'd saved the boys from a fate worse than death. They'd be home before they knew it, and with no fleet the Pirate King would be unable to reach them before the Bloodmoon had passed. Yet a kernel of doubt settled in her mind. The Pirate King didn't need a ship – he could control the creatures of the sea; the burning ache of missing Padre flared inside as she recalled the giant squid.

'Care for a dance?' Felipe asked, extending his hand towards her.

She pushed the doubt to one side and let a smile spread across her face. The boys on the deck danced and cheered as the crew sang sea shanties whilst busying themselves with riggings and ropes. She longed to share in their undiluted happiness. She didn't want to think about the Pirate King or the prophecy, or the magic which had flashed beneath her hands. Right now, all she wanted was to dance with her friend. And this was going to be so much better than dancing with Salvador.

Gradually, the day blurred into night and the moon appeared: a giant opal in the sky. *Soon it will turn red*, Tiggy thought, as relief flourished throughout her body. *The Pirate King is nowhere to be seen. Maybe we really have escaped.*

Diego slipped his hand inside hers and they gazed at the stars, which blinked in the dark like fireflies.

'Will Madre save me some whipped sugar from the carnival?' he asked.

'I'll make you some myself,' she replied, ruffling his hair.

Just then, a loud noise – deeper than whale song, heavier than thunder – slashed through the air. Something snapped inside Tiggy's heart: the taut string which had only just managed to hold her grief at bay. It was the same noise she had heard at the beach when Padre was cruelly wrenched from her.

Another cry reverberated through her boots as she searched the ocean. Sure enough, a monstrous, shining head was emerging from the waves, less than half a fathom away.

The giant squid.

The tentacles came first, thrashing like enormous eels, followed by the pitch of its huge body. The boys stopped dancing, the crew froze, ropes slipping through their fingers. Lucia leapt on to the railings, eyeglass pressed to her face. 'Kraken, save us,' she said.

The squid threw open its tentacles and unfolded its cavernous beak. Just as Tiggy had feared, balanced on its giant tongue was the Pirate King and a handful of his toughest men, Snake-hair and Brute included. Tiggy's head reeled, her hands instinctively reached for Diego and she pulled him behind her, watching in horror as the mage harnessed his turquoise light and sliced the image of a claw into the air before him.

Carried on the breeze, she heard the word: *Attarque.*

A strange noise crept into the air, similar to the spider crabs and giant lobsters who had stolen her brother from her only days ago: a *rat-a-tat* of claws against the hull, growing in strength until the entire galleon seemed to shake with the sound of gunfire. All at once, hundreds of rock crabs swarmed on to the decks, transforming the planks into a red-orange ripple as they snapped their pincers and darted towards the boys.

The boys scattered, some of them heading on to the higher decks, some grabbing up oars and swiping at the little beasts. Tiggy felt a sharp nip on her ankle and kicked the creature away, trying not to hurt it too badly; the crabs were, after all, not acting of their own free will. Diego yelped at her side, so Tiggy swept him into her arms, lifting him free of the little blighters.

'Look, Tig,' Diego said. 'They're snipping the

ropes.' Sure enough, the crabs had begun dismantling the rigging with whirring claws.

'They must be trying to stop us escaping,' she replied, then, turning to Marina, she asked, 'Can you sing again? Put the mage to sleep?'

Marina shook her head. 'I . . . I don't know. The castle has left me pretty tired. I can try.'

Cannon arrived on deck, pink in the face and panting. 'Captain, I used all me cannons in the cave.'

Lucia leapt from her post, drawing her sword with gusto. 'There's no way we can outsail that squid.'

The squid was now close enough that Tiggy could see individual suckers, stippled and pink against the dark underbelly of the tentacles. She had to do something, but what? She was a mage too, Clara had insisted, but she had no idea how to use her powers to save them. Self-doubt washed over her. She'd already done so many things which yesterday had seemed impossible, yet defeating the Pirate King – the most powerful mage ever to have lived – seemed ever out of reach.

A massive tentacle hovered over the galleon, cutting from moonlight a long shadow upon the deck. The crew began to fire, but the creature didn't even notice the onslaught of bullets as they flashed turquoise across its skin. A few of the smaller boys began to cry. Tiggy dragged Diego from the railings to avoid him being struck, positioning her body between the boy and the assault.

Yet when the squid lowered its tentacle against the side of the galleon, it did so with care and precision.

It wasn't an attack, it was a gangplank.

The Pirate King was going to board.

CHAPTER 37

The Pirate King hauled himself from the squid's tongue on to its tentacle, and ambled towards the galleon as if he was taking his daily stroll. He reached the railing and dropped on to the planks below, a curious smile dancing across his arrogant face. His men then filed from the tentacle on to the galleon. They stood, faces fierce, weapons raised and ready to strike, yet the Pirate King simply brushed down his fitted jacket and readjusted his tricorn hat, as if preparing for dinner, not war.

Marina lifted her necklace and attempted to sing

– but her voice emerged a wavering croak and the necklace remained dull. She was right. Her powers had withered. Realizing this, Miguel ran at the Pirate King with his dagger raised, followed by a roaring Doc, but the mage dismissed them with a mere flick of his hand – turquoise light zipped around Tiggy's friends' chests and knocked them to the floor. The pair struggled into a sitting position, rubbing their heads.

'Hold your ground,' Lucia commanded, her sword aimed at the Pirate King.

The mage pointed to Felipe. 'So, you're the boy who will reawaken the curse.' Magic fizzed between his fingers and the threat of violence seemed to coat the air. 'The very boy who helped my mermaid escape back at the castle.' He smiled. 'Oh yes, I shall enjoy killing you when the Bloodmoon finally appears.'

'No!' Marina gasped.

Tiggy stepped forwards, pulling herself tall even though she felt smaller than the crabs which scampered around her feet. 'Wait, I'm—'

The Pirate King cut across her, his attention focused entirely on Felipe. 'But for now, a binding spell should ensure you don't escape again.' He threaded his fingers through the air, drawing a long, shimmering rope. '*Restrangler*,' he whispered, as he fired the turquoise rope towards Felipe.

Before she had time to speak or even think, Tiggy stepped between the turquoise light and Felipe, her hands raised, her face scrunched as she anticipated the whip of sorcery across her skin. But she felt nothing. Only a stirring of something fresh and cool inside her stomach. The turquoise rope dissolved against her palms and the onlookers gasped.

Tiggy steadied her voice and squared her shoulders. 'I am the child from the prophecy.'

The Pirate King froze, his face fixed in a scowl. Then a sudden laugh burst from his mouth, causing Tiggy to jump. 'Impossible!' he said, a cruel smirk settling on his face. 'It can't be you. After all, you're just a *girl*.'

She took a deep breath. 'There is no such thing as *just* a girl,' she replied defiantly.

Snake-hair piped up. 'Seriously, boss, did you see the way she dissolved your magic?'

The other pirates nodded.

'Brute,' Brute said, agreeing wholeheartedly.

The Pirate King spun to face his men. 'ENOUGH!' he roared. His face reddened and he clenched his fists.

His men shuffled apologetically, casting their eyes downward, and the Pirate King focused his attention on Tiggy, sauntering towards her until they were almost nose to nose.

Tiggy could feel his foul breath on her skin; she could see every line of his face – a map of rage and cruelty. She wanted to flinch, to step away, but she gathered her strength and stood completely still.

Ever so slowly, he studied her face, his eyes seeming to bore into her own. 'Yes,' he eventually whispered. 'You have the sorcery of the waves in you, don't you? Good job I found you before you learnt to use it.' He strode to the side of the ship and pointed to the moon, leaving Tiggy to draw in a few quick breaths. 'In a few moments, it won't matter. The sacrifice will be made, the curse will reawaken and I will have my army back.' His voice climbed higher and higher. 'And then nobody will stop me. I will rule *everything*.' He punched his fist in the air and blue light forked from his fingers like upside-down lightning.

His men began to clap and cheer.

'Is this guy for real?' Felipe hissed to Marina.

The Pirate King swung round, suspicion locked into his face. He glanced at Marina and his dark eyes flashed a vivid blue – magic acknowledging magic. 'Ah, yes. The selkie who sang so beautifully at the castle. I lost my mermaid, thanks to you, so it seems only fitting that I drink *your* blood instead.'

He clicked his fingers and a group of his pirates surrounded Marina, snatching her sealskin cloak and wrenching her hands behind her back.

Marina released a muffled scream and panic clamoured in Tiggy's heart.

'Stop!' Tiggy cried, before adding more gently, 'Please, don't do this. I know you're still mad because of what the Islanders did to your madre, but please, don't take it out on these children.' She gestured to Marina and the crowd of boys. 'They're all innocent.'

But the Pirate King would not relent. 'So was my madre,' he whispered.

The deep rumble of cannon fire drew their attention. Tiggy turned to see a fleet of galleons moving towards them at speed, their sails filled with wind and courage. She let out a shuddering breath.

'The Navy,' Lucia shouted. 'The Navy of the Fortune Isles is approaching.'

'Clara,' Felipe whispered, his voice flecked with hope. 'She must have fetched help.'

'They're too late,' the Pirate King said. He stepped

forward and clutched Tiggy's face, tightening his grip so that red-hot pain radiated from his fingers. 'Come, little sorceress, your destiny awaits.' He adjusted his grip and began dragging her by the hair to the bow of the galleon. Through a fug of pain, she heard Diego squeal, Felipe and the crew trying to help, but she knew they were no match for the Pirate King's men.

Then everything seemed to stop. The boys, the crew, the pirates. Even the waves froze.

Silence fell.

Tiggy looked up, her head throbbing with hurt and terror. A scarlet patch had appeared on the side of the moon as if it were injured. *The Bloodmoon, it's actually happening*, she thought. And within the beat of a heart, the moon transformed into a crimson sphere, bathing everything in a devilish glow. Cries and gasps escaped from the boys of Haven, for hell itself had surely opened, pouring its fire into the sky.

'The Bloodmoon,' the Pirate King whispered, his eyes alight.

As if recognizing his voice, the waves began to churn again, reflecting the crimson above so the ocean became like a giant pool of blood.

'Come.' The Pirate King continued to drag his sacrifice across the deck. 'It is time.'

Tiggy saw the break in the railings and finally realized her fate: she was going to walk the plank.

The Pirate King pressed the tip of a blade into her back and she was forced to stumble on to the thin length of wood, her vision swimming with terror. She risked glancing below and saw the flash of fins and teeth. The mage had summoned sharks! Her legs seemed to buckle and she very nearly toppled overboard without even a flicker of magic as she stumbled along its length.

The Pirate King smiled, and then began swiping his light-filled hands through the air. He glanced at the moon – a wound in the sky – and began reciting the prophecy. With every word, he sliced his hands through the night, drawing the shape of a turquoise dagger.

'*Beneath the Bloodmoon, the curse shall be saved,*
An army of Golems shall rise from the grave,
When a child of Haven, born of a wave,
Falls at the hand of the deadliest Mage.'

Fully formed, the dagger sizzled between them.

The Pirate King raised his hands, ready to strike, his mocking face turned scarlet by the blaze of the moon.

'No,' Tiggy heard a woman cry. 'Stop . . . please, you don't know who she is.'

The Pirate King paused. One of the Naval galleons had drawn near, and leaning from its bow was a woman with long dark hair whipping across her urgent expression.

Tiggy's stomach somersaulted and her head filled with a jumble of confusion and joy.

The woman on the bow was Madre.

CHAPTER 38

'You have to stop. You have no idea who this girl is,' Madre cried.

'She is the child from the prophecy,' the Pirate King bellowed back. 'What more do I need to know?'

Madre's entire body seemed to sag against the railings of her galleon. 'Listen to me, please,' she shouted. 'You had a child once, many, many years ago, and this girl is your bloodline. Your great- great-great-granddaughter.'

The crew gasped. The Pirate King faltered; the

hatred slipped from his face, replaced by an expression of shock and uncertainty. Time seemed to slow. Tiggy felt completely numb, as if she'd been held in ice water for several hours . . . how could this . . . this *fiend* be related to her?

The turquoise dagger dissolved in the air, and finally, beckoning towards Madre, trailing light from the tips of his fingers, the Pirate King spoke: *Levari*. The squid moved through the water like a small, glossy mountain, before reaching Madre's galleon and extending a tentacle towards her. Without hesitation, without a quiver of fear, Madre hitched up her skirt and climbed aboard the tentacle, allowing the squid to carry her across to Tiggy's galleon.

Madre scrambled safely on board, helped by Lucia and Felipe, and then hugged an overjoyed Diego. Slowly, anxiety gnawing at her features, she turned to face Tiggy.

Tiggy wobbled on her plank, tears winding down her cheeks. She had missed her mother so much. 'Madre?' she whispered. 'Are we really related to this . . . this . . . beast?'

Something quivered below Madre's features, something Tiggy couldn't quite place. Sadness?

Guilt? And instead of replying, Madre turned her attention towards the Pirate King. 'Please. Let me pull her back to safety. Then I will explain everything.'

The Pirate King grinned a wicked grin, the mask of hatred firmly reapplied to his face. He stepped away from the plank in one smooth stride. 'Why no, Señora. Why don't you join her? You can explain yourself just as well hovering over my hungry sharks.' He glanced at the scarlet moon. 'I'm really rather curious, but we don't have long – the sacrifice should be taken by the sea, under the Bloodmoon – so please be quick.'

Diego shrieked, clinging to the folds of his mother's skirts. Madre's face tightened, her lips pressed together in a thin line, but after pecking Diego on the forehead, she passed him to Felipe and nodded.

'No, please,' Tiggy whispered, yet Madre was already easing on to the plank with tentative steps. Tiggy could smell the familiar scent of home catching on the breeze – rosewater, fresh bread and laurel – and it felt like she'd swallowed something long and sharp. She longed to run to Madre, to hold her close and weep like she was five, but the teeth and fins still glinted in her peripheral vision, and she was afraid to unsettle the flimsy extension of wood which separated her and Madre from a painful death.

Madre fixed her with large, tear-drenched eyes. 'Oh, Tiggy, we've been looking for you and the boys since yesterday, just sailing around praying for a miracle. And then a miracle arrived in the form of a mermaid.'

'Clara,' Tiggy whispered softly. 'She's called Clara.'

Madre nodded, a large tear plopping from her chin. 'All these years I've longed to tell you. Please forgive me for keeping secrets.' She took a deep breath. 'Your *birth* madre was descended from the Pirate King. Not me.'

Tiggy squinted, her head battered with confusion, her thoughts slowly unravelling. 'But you're my madre.'

'I am, of course I am, and you are my daughter. But by blood, Tiggy, I am not your madre. I was friends with your mother when she visited land, but I only married your padre after your birth madre was lost at sea.'

Tiggy could hear the words, and yet it was as though they'd lost all meaning, as though a thin film of shock had fallen between her and Madre, preventing any sense from reaching her. 'You're not my birth madre?' The sentence dried in her mouth.

Madre shook her head – a sad tremble. 'After your birth mother fell for a landlubber, your padre, she had you, Antigua.' She sniffed. 'But the call of the ocean was too strong, and your mother couldn't resist it, even though she tried. She knew the danger of the sea and made me promise to help raise you if she never returned. And she was right to worry, for months passed with no word, and eventually we accepted that the sea had claimed her. I kept my word and cared for you as if you were my own, though I had no idea I would fall in love with your padre.' Madre managed a sad smile. 'Eventually, we married and had Diego. We became a family, Antigua, though we always hoped your birth mother would one day return. I'm so sorry we never told you the truth.' Her voice cracked and her body seemed to lurch forwards from the weight of the confession. 'I didn't want you to think you were destined to turn out like *him*.' She gestured to the Pirate King.

Questions clamoured in Tiggy's head, so many she didn't know where to start. The world as she knew it was crashing in around her and she began to feel like she too was falling apart. 'Did you know the Pirate King was alive?' she asked in a small voice.

Madre bit her lip, deep in thought. 'It was always a concern,' she eventually said.

Tiggy realized that these were the secrets Madre had discussed with Gabriella back at the tavern. Her hand covered her mouth as another realization hit her: it was her birth madre who owed Benito an eye. 'How many other people know?' she asked, unable to stop the bite of anger in her words.

'Not many, I promise. Gabriella knew because she was friends with your birth madre too.'

'The trials of the ocean,' Tiggy whispered. 'Is this what she meant? That I must face my . . . my . . . evil great-great-great-grandfather, the Pirate King.'

Madre nodded. 'She always shared my worry.' Her bottom lip began to quiver and she looked as if she might lose her footing. Tiggy crossed the plank in a few easy strides, not caring that the sharks slid below, caring only that she steadied her mother before she tumbled into the treacherous waves. Madre fell into her arms and began to gasp. 'Oh, Tiggy. That's why I was so hard on you, why I wanted you to stay away from the ocean, because I was terrified you'd end up like your birth mother, or worse, the Pirate King. I didn't want the sorcery to awaken within you.'

The plank began to wobble, causing the blood-thirsty sharks to circle even quicker, their blade-sharp teeth rearing from the water. In the background, Tiggy could hear Diego's cries, her friends begging the Pirate King to allow her and Madre back on board.

'It's OK,' Tiggy whispered into Madre's hair, even as her stomach churned and the ragged blade of sorrow sawed at her chest.

Her birth mother was dead.

Her father was dead.

She was an orphan.

She looked over Madre's shoulder towards the Pirate King. Surely he wouldn't harm her now, his own flesh and blood. Surely even the Pirate King wouldn't sink so low. As if reading her thoughts, his face hardened, the tendons protruding from his neck like iron rods. For a terrible moment, Tiggy thought he would wield his magic like a whip, slicing her and Madre from the plank with one brutal command. Yet slowly, he sketched another dagger in the air, the turquoise vivid against the blush of the sky. 'It makes perfect sense, little sorceress. Of course you are the sacrifice. It simply had to be you.'

'Why?' Antigua whispered.

He held the dagger steady, his voice rising with zeal. 'Because the ocean shall have only one King.'

And with that, he shoved the dagger of light deep towards Tiggy and Madre's chests.

CHAPTER 39

Before they could react, before they could even scream, they tumbled from the plank straight into the midst of those waiting teeth. The water sucked them under, forcing the breath from their lungs. Tiggy reached helplessly for Madre, only to feel the slippery skin of the sharks; a spike of terror stabbed at her heart. Thrashing and twisting beneath the surface like a wounded fish, the final lines of the prophecy sounded in her head like an alarm: *A child of Haven, born of a wave, falls at the hand of the deadliest Mage.*

It was over.

She would die, the only madre she had ever known would die too, the boys would transform into Sea Golems and her best friend would be drained of her blood. In one final desperate bid for survival, she broke the surface of the water, gasping, flailing, surrounded by fins and sea-froth. Madre appeared beside her, hacking up brine and desperately treading water.

A line of boys peered over the railing of the galleon, watching them with pity and fear in their eyes, the light of the moon reddening their cheeks.

'Diego,' Madre managed to gurgle.

Tiggy began hunting for him, desperate to see his sweet face one last time before life was ripped from her and his form changed for ever. She opened her mouth to yell his name, when the air was filled with a deafening scream – the collective call of hundreds of boys in pain.

The Pirate King laughed. His hand flashed and the sharks retreated a little, swimming a lazy circle around Tiggy and Madre. 'The curse has awakened already, Antigua. Seems I didn't need to kill you after all, only defeat you. How delightful. This way you get to watch, and *then* my sharks will rip you limb from limb.'

And watch she did, her head filled with pain and dismay, as the boys above her began to change. Jagged cones bulged from their faces like giant boils and their skin became toad-like and caked with ocean clay. Their eyes grew black and unblinking as green, weedy tendrils sprouted from their heads. Their fingers, still gripping the railings, grew long and webbed.

'No, please no,' Tiggy spluttered, as the Pirate King's hand flashed once more.

And just before the jaws of a hungry shark closed around her calf, yanking her beneath the waves, she saw the face of her little brother, twisted in pain as barnacles sprouted across his cheeks.

CHAPTER 40

Tiggy rocketed down, down, down. Her lungs contracted, crushed with pressure, and her head felt as though it would rip clean from her body. Then she seemed to pause, suspended beneath the waves, her heart pummelling in her chest and her vision smudged with salt and fear. A rush of pain screamed up her leg as the shark bore down on her ankle. She kicked at it, but ended up just flailing in the water. Drawn by the scent of her blood, more sharks dived towards her – a troop of jagged fins and snapping jaws. *At least they will leave Madre be*, Tiggy thought.

Her ears rang and her lungs burnt a hole in her chest, yet somehow, driven by pure panic, she remembered the small dagger hidden safely inside her pocket. It was her only chance. So focusing beyond the pain, she pulled it free and pressed the tiny button to release the blade. Frantically, she sliced the little knife through the water, trying to free her leg from the snare of teeth.

But it was no use.

The shark was too strong, and pain coursed up her left arm as another set of snarling jaws fastened on to her hand.

She twisted and turned, spinning desperately in the water, unsure which way was up or down, jabbing manically with her weapon. More sharks lunged. Her mouth yawned into a silent scream and salt water streamed down her throat, filling her lungs with molten pain.

She gasped and gagged all at once.

More molten pain.

There was no escape.

Her heart strained. The world began to fade. Her thoughts blurred into nothing.

She gulped one last mouthful of water, before her lungs gave up completely and her brave, brave heart ground to a halt.

CHAPTER 41

Clara arrived to see the girl sinking amidst a swarm of hungry sharks. Without a second to lose, the mermaid shot through the attackers like a violet harpoon, scattering them with her mighty tail. The girl now floated before her like an abandoned doll, arms extended, blood spooling from teeth marks on her ankle and hand. Was she dead? No. Clara refused to believe it. Determinedly, she scooped the limp body into hers and felt for a pulse which wasn't there. But when the mermaid's fingers touched Tiggy's neck, she felt a flicker of something

beneath her skin, just like she did back at the castle –
the girl still had magic.

A flicker of life remained.

Yet how could Clara save her? A simple healing
hex couldn't restore life. The mermaid threw
back her head, exasperated. She *had* to do
something. Suddenly the sight of Tiggy's blood
awoke an idea – the Pirate King had used mermaid's
blood to heal himself to bring himself back from
the brink of death, so perhaps it could heal Tiggy
too.

Spying the small blade still clutched between
Tiggy's fingers, Clara prised it free and nicked her
own palm. A ribbon of blood wound its way towards
the surface and she winced as pain flashed up her
wrist. She then clutched Tiggy's injured hand with
her own. The familiar buzz of ocean magic
resonated through her body as her own blood mixed
with the young mage's. The two girls faced one
another, floating within the water, and the blood
which spiralled from their connected palms
coloured the surrounding ocean with inky-blue
fronds.

Tiggy's eyes began to flutter, her mouth twitched.
Clara grinned. *That's it, Antigua de Fortune. You*

can do it. She leant forward and released a lungful of air into Tiggy's mouth.

And very slowly Tiggy opened her eyes.

CHAPTER 42

The first emotion which hit Tiggy as the world swam back into focus wasn't relief or gratitude, but deep confusion. She had died. She was sure of it. Attacked by sharks and drowned by the sea, destined to join the Army of Lost Souls and relive her final moments again and again. But when Clara's face grinned back at her, she realized that the breath in her lungs wasn't her own. She glanced at her ankle and hand and saw that her wounds had closed.

Clara had saved her.

Her mouth fell open in disbelief – a large bubble passed before her eyes. Before she could express her thanks, fear gripped at her stomach and flipped it upside down. Had the sharks claimed Madre too?

Clara's voice sounded in her head, loud and clear as though she were speaking directly into her ear. *Don't worry. The mage set the sharks only on you. My padre has taken your mother to the surface, away from any danger.*

The relief was short-lived, the image of Diego transforming into a Golem still hot and raw. Tiggy may have returned from the edge of death, Madre safe, but the Pirate King had still won.

Who says he's won? Clara asked, reading her thoughts.

The curse has awakened, Tiggy replied silently. *The boys are turning into Sea Golems. I saw it with my own eyes.*

Look to the surface, Clara said. *What do you see?*

In the distance, Tiggy saw the collection of galleons hanging like oblong storm clouds against a crimson sky. The sharks had vanished, and beyond the surface she saw the burning embers of a night sky, still bathed in blood. *The Bloodmoon*, she replied. *It's still there.*

Clara smiled. *And do you think you've fallen, Antigua de Fortune?*

She heard Padre's words from the ball the other night: *It doesn't matter that you fall. What matters is you stand again.*

Clara grinned. *Your padre was a wise man.* With that, the mermaid began shooting upwards, sweeping Tiggy towards the galleon in a cloud of bubbles. And just before they reached the surface, the pair stopped, shielded beneath the hull of the Pirate King's galleon. Clara faced her, determination sparking in her eyes. *There's still time, Antigua. So long as the Bloodmoon burns and your heart still beats, there's still time. Now stand and fight.*

Yet Tiggy noticed that the mermaid's voice sounded further and further away, as if an entire ocean rolled between them, her violet scales smudging across her face as reality dovetailed into unconsciousness. She was running out of oxygen again. *Please, Clara, I need some more of your air.*

Clara shook her head. *Not this time, Antigua. This time, you breathe yourself.*

Confused, Tiggy glanced to the surface – she could just about make it. Yet as she tried to pull away, Clara's grip intensified.

Tiggy kicked her legs, panic shooting through her body. *Please, Clara. I'm going to drown.*

Clara held her tight. *Breathe, Antigua, breathe.*

I can't . . . it's impossible, Tiggy replied.

Clara smiled, her violet eyes burning with promise. *Everything is impossible, until it happens.*

And because she couldn't break free, because her lungs could no longer resist the urge to suck, and because her trust in the mermaid was strong, Tiggy finally drew breath.

As expected, a huge mouthful of salt water forced its way into her lungs, stinging her chest as if she'd swallowed a jellyfish – the exact same molten pain she'd felt when surrounded by the sharks. Yet this time, facing Clara, a surge of magic cooling her veins, she felt strangely calm.

Clara nodded. *Never fear the ocean, Antigua de Fortune, for you are its rightful Queen.*

Tiggy inhaled another mouthful of brine. It felt cooling, like the early morning sea air which trundled on to the shore. Her lungs kept sucking, greedy for more; she inhaled another chestful, then another and another. Gradually, the fog lifted from her mind and her vision returned. She found she could move her hands, her limbs, and the noises of the ocean sharpened in her ears. She looked at Clara and laughed, bubbles bursting from her lips. She could breathe underwater.

Clara squealed with delight, her voice now as clear as a bell in Tiggy's mind. *That's it, Tiggy.*

Submerged in the ocean, surrounded by shafts of sunlight and shoals of fish, the distant boom of whale song and the click of dolphins, Tiggy felt the magic bloom inside her like never before. That wonderful cool tingle started in her belly, followed by the sensation of lapping waves undulating through her entire body, and finally an explosion of salt and spray right inside her heart. She stretched her hands before her, watching as dark-blue ink billowed from her fingertips, lighting up the surrounding water so she and Clara hung suspended in a shimmering, turquoise bubble.

It's time, Clara said. *Command the ocean like I know you can.*

Tiggy smiled. *I don't need to command the ocean*, she told the mermaid. *I need to* become *the ocean.*

Clara nodded, her pointed teeth gleaming in the aquamarine glow. *I believe you are right, Antigua de Fortune of the High Seas.*

CHAPTER 43

Tiggy swam beneath the galleon with surprising ease, her hands leaving trails of inky-blue magic in the waters behind her. She had never felt so buoyant, so free; she was flying in the sea like a gull in the sky. She broke the surface of the ocean and noticed with relief that the Bloodmoon still glowed as brightly as ever.

Raising her hands, she saw streams of water spiralling from her palms, connecting her to the sea as though it really were an extension of her. Instinctively, Tiggy knew what to do, and lifted her hands even higher so she created a pillar of water. It spun before her like a small tower, froth dancing on its peak.

'No!' a voice boomed. She looked up to see the Pirate King staring at her, his face jagged with anger. 'It can't be.'

Tiggy didn't reply, she simply scooped her hands low and raised them upwards as though conducting an orchestra. The ocean complied, seeming to hug her legs and form a thick mast of water beneath her. Slowly, Tiggy rose into the air, suspended on a column of sea.

A joyous laugh fell from her mouth. All her life she had dreamt of an ocean life, and now she was a sorceress of the sea. It was beyond her wildest dreams, and the excitement shone inside her like a sun.

Yet the sight which met her eyes as she looked down upon the Pirate King's galleon dissolved her newly found confidence in an instant. A swarm of half-Golems writhed upon the decks, clutching at their faces in agony, any evidence of their humanity almost gone. The boys of Haven had almost completely transformed. Panic blasted through Tiggy's chest as she stared at their slimy green bodies, their spindly limbs and webbed feet. One of those beasts was her darling brother, and one was Felipe – she simply couldn't bear it.

The Pirate King seized his chance to gain the upper hand. 'Do you know how I turn them into Golems?'

'Magic,' she replied, her voice hollow.

'Well, yes. Obviously.' He smirked. 'I extract their souls, and send them down into Davy Jones's locker, Antigua. And then I fill their vacant bodies with my will. My magic.'

Tiggy wobbled on her tower of water, all her self-assurance leeching away. 'No,' she whispered, searching the squirming sea beasts for her brother.

'Once that process is complete,' the Pirate King continued, 'I will have my army of Sea Golems, and they will never be boys again.'

Once that process is complete . . .

So, it wasn't done yet. Tiggy felt her hopes rise, and then evaporate as she cast around for a solution. She had no idea how to catch a boy's soul.

'Tiggy, think.' Marina shouted up to her. 'He's sending their souls to Davy Jones's locker, which means they must be in the—' Her sentence finished abruptly as Brute slapped his spade-like hand over her mouth. But it was enough for Tiggy to understand. If the boys' souls were being sent to Davy Jones's locker, then they must be *in the ocean*.

She lowered herself so that the waters engulfed her legs, and dipped her hands into the waves. Then, closing her eyes, she let the cool tingle of magic crawl up her arms and into her heart and sent her awareness *down*. That was when she sensed them: dark shapes slipping between the fish and seaweed and flecks of sand, a shoal of shadows travelling towards the ocean floor.

The Pirate King's voice cut through her thoughts. 'Poor girl, you have so much to learn. Even I can't summon souls back from the ocean. They are gone. I have my army. Accept defeat – and perhaps I can start to teach you what you *can* do . . .'

Tiggy pushed the voice aside – and the doubts that swirled with them. She squeezed her eyes even tighter and focused on the shadows. Hundreds of memories began unfolding inside her like blossom as she connected with each soul. She heard lullabies, the sound of a school bell and children playing, she tasted fresh crab, pickled eggs and sticky date pudding, she felt the embrace of the madres and padres of Haven, the soft fold of quilts at night, and saw the sun sinking into the ocean, leaving just a smattering of stars.

'Come back,' she whispered to the boys. 'Come back.'

But they didn't stop . . . *couldn't* stop.

Then, within the throng, she fell upon the scent of laurel, of freshly baked bread and tin soldiers, the brush of fur from a one-eyed bear. She had found Diego.

She clutched at the memories and lifted her hands with all her might.

But again, nothing happened. The souls continued to sink, faster and faster towards the ocean bed.

'It's useless,' the Pirate King taunted. 'They are mine – and the ocean is too!'

Tiggy didn't feel scared; she didn't let herself. Everything is impossible, until it happens. She turned to the waves which stretched into for ever, and reached deep into her heart. There, at her very core, she found something warm and beating. Something which called to mind playing at stacking stones with Diego, snuggling with her family around an open hearth whilst the cold rattled the windows in their panes, nature walks with Padre, bedtime stories under the quilt with Madre and family feasts of freshly caught fish.

She found love, held in the palm of an ink-soft hand. Love for Madre, for Diego, her friends . . . love for her darling Padre, who would always be present in her soul. She drew strength from this love, allowing it to fill her being with warmth and joy. Then she wove it together with the cool beauty of the ocean sorcery, so tightly that magic and love became one.

Whereas the Pirate King had bound his magic to hate, she would bind hers to love.

Something shifted beneath her. The dark shapes seemed to pause, hovering, their downwards motion interrupted.

Purposefully, she raised her hands high above her, allowing the magic to move through her veins.

And the impossible happened. The souls began travelling upwards, moving quicker than ever before, twisting and lurching towards the surface. Before Tiggy could even breathe, she felt the water around her thrum with life as hundreds of willowy blue flames burst from the surface, catching in the light of the Bloodmoon, spinning, dancing, sweeping back towards the galleon. She laughed, the hairs on the back of her neck stirring as though brushed by a hundred invisible fingers.

'What's happening?' The Pirate King roared as the blue flames rushed towards the half-Golems on the deck. 'This is impossible! I am the ocean's King!'

'Everything is impossible, until it happens.' Tiggy stretched upwards on her tower of water, feeling as though she had grown thick salty legs, feeling her footing right on the bottom of the ocean floor. She had the weight of an entire sea behind her: nothing and no one could stop her now.

CHAPTER 44

Carefully, trying not to tremble, she allowed the ocean to lower her on to the deck of the galleon. The wood met her feet, sturdy and real, and she finally allowed the exhaustion to claim her, crumpling to the ground with a thud. Marina and the crew rushed towards her.

'Tiggy. Oh, Tiggy, you're OK,' Marina cried.

Through the flicker of her eyelids, Tiggy could just make out the blue flames diving back into the half-Golems which writhed on the deck. The Golems stilled, and their transformation began to reverse: the barnacles and seaweed retreated into their faces as quickly as it arrived, their spindly limbs grew fleshy and plump once more and their spines straightened. It was a quick process, yet it filled Tiggy's aching heart with joy.

She felt her strength return as she watched them stand. Their clothes were bedraggled, their hair matted with sea clay, yet their faces shone bright with excitement and relief. They were boys again. They began checking their hands and feet, then hugging one another, whoops of joy sparking in the night.

Her eyes darted across the crowded galleon, searching for a glimpse of her little brother. 'Diego?' she whispered. And, as if he heard, he appeared, breaking from the crowd and dashing towards her, Bobo still clutched to his chest, not even a trace of barnacles on his face. 'You did it, Tig,' he squealed, bending to hug her. 'You saved us.'

Tears of joy leaked down her cheeks, and she let Diego and Marina help her back to her feet.

She held her little brother at arm's length, looking him up and down, checking for injuries. 'Diego, praise Kraken, are you OK?'

He grinned. 'OK? Of course I'm OK. That was ... that was ... AWESOME!'

Felipe appeared by their side. A clump of dried mud still stuck in his hair, the only clue that moments ago he had almost been a Sea Golem. 'Where's the Pirate King?' he asked.

The delight splintered for a moment. Tiggy and her friends looked frantically across the deck. But the mage was nowhere to be seen.

'There,' Lucia screamed. She was standing on the ship's beakhead, pointing angrily to the waves below. 'That sea weasel is trying to escape, do you see, Antigua?'

Hurtling away from them was the head of the giant squid.

'You have to stop him,' Marina cried. 'Or he'll wait till the next Bloodmoon and do it again.'

Marina was right. Tiggy had to stop him. She held the squid in her sights and felt the sorcery flourish and grow inside her – she no longer needed to touch the ocean to draw upon its power. It ran in her veins. 'Not so fast, Great-grandad,' she whispered through gritted teeth. Then gathering her skill, she let the rolling of the waves move through her, the taste of salt form on her tongue, the sound of the gulls and the turning tide fill her head, and firmly she raised a hand over the edge of the ship.

The water below seemed to fill with soft, inky magic, an indigo paint which leeched across the surface of the water with long, spidery fingers. Faster and faster, it stretched towards the giant squid, like a blue-black crevasse splitting the earth in two.

Tiggy's magic surrounded the squid, a ring of navy, and the squid paused.

The boys gasped and the crew cheered.

'You stopped the squid,' Marina squeaked.

They all watched, transfixed, as the squid slowly turned to face them, raising its head above the water-ledge so its gaze met Tiggy's.

Tiggy felt surprisingly calm. 'It's time to be free,' she told it gently.

The turquoise light which sizzled in its eyes faded, and very slowly it opened its mouth to reveal the Pirate King standing upon its tongue.

The mage stared at Tiggy with hard, relentless eyes, his skin tinged with the red of the Bloodmoon. He raised his voice, though she noticed it sounded far less commanding now he was attempting to escape. 'You may destroy me,' he called. 'But you will never be King.'

Tiggy simply smiled. 'Oh, Great-grandfather, when will you learn? The ocean shall have no king.'

And with that, the squid let out an almighty roar and spat the Pirate King into the ocean like a piece of chewed-up fish.

Tiggy and her friends leant over the railings and watched as the ocean sucked the Pirate King beneath the waves. The turquoise glow whirled between his fingers as he desperately tried to summon help, but the sharks which had bowed to his command only moments ago now pummelled towards him, teeth bared, chasing him further into the salty gloom. And just before he vanished entirely, the turquoise glow of his sorcery fading for ever, the colourful wisps of an army of mermaids swarmed around him, dragging him deeper and deeper down.

CHAPTER 45

our weeks later

By nightfall, a carnival adorned the beach. Colourful stalls made from striped linen filled the spaces between the mechanical fairground rides, strings of lanterns criss-crossed overhead, draped between unspeakably tall wooden poles, and townsfolk dressed as mermaids and sea creatures tottered around on stilts, handing out whistles and flags to excited children.

Tiggy watched Diego as he skipped ahead, his

eyes desperately searching for whipped sugar, his nose sniffing the air like a hound. The strident notes of the brass band mixed with the whir of cogs from the mechanical pirate ship and the screams of the thrill seekers who rode it. She let the scent of baked goods and roasted eels fill her nostrils and smiled to herself.

A man on stilts leant towards her, a grin lighting up his painted face. 'For you, Guardian.' He presented her with a single red rose.

'Thank you.' She tucked it behind her ear, enjoying the brush of petals against her cheek, and continued after her little brother, who'd paused, momentarily distracted by a Punch and Judy show. Only it wasn't Punch and Judy – it was Tiggy and the Pirate King, and puppet-Tiggy was walloping her opponent over the head with a mini-club whilst shouting, 'You're not the king, you're a very naughty boy.'

'I'm sorry, Guardian of the Ocean,' the puppet-villain said, cowering beneath his tiny cloth arms.

Tiggy still couldn't get used to her new title. *Guardian of the Ocean.* It sounded so grand, so responsible. All the same, she couldn't help but laugh as an army of miniature merfolk stitched from bright rags overwhelmed the Pirate King and dragged him beneath a painted cardboard sea.

Over the cheers of the children, she heard Marina and Felipe calling, 'Tig, Tig, there you are!'

They ran towards her, their faces alight. Their unusually smart clothes were already speckled with sand and dollops of melted chocolate, giving Marina's light-blue cotton dress the impression of a bird's egg. Her winkle charm glinted around her neck with pride: she no longer needed to hide her selkie roots from the eyes of the townsfolk, not since she'd played such a vital role in saving the Haven boys.

'Well, Diego,' Marina said. 'What do you think? It's four weeks late, but it's finally here – the Blood-moon Carnival.'

'Minus the Bloodmoon,' Felipe quipped. 'Praise Kraken.'

'It's the best thing ever,' Diego said, hopping up and down, excitement bubbling out of him. 'Even better than being a Sea Golem.'

'Diego, the Pirate King was trying to steal your soul,' Marina scolded.

Diego pointed defiantly to his chin. 'I had barnacles on my face, Mari. Barnacles!'

Marina sighed, clearly irate.

'Silly guppy,' Tiggy said, ruffling her brother's hair. 'Come on, let's go find that candyfloss before the ceremony – Madre made me triple promise I wouldn't be late.'

The friends drifted between the stalls, taking in the colourful activities: children tossing hoops on to sticks, knocking coconuts from their stands with shiny balls and fishing wooden gulls from a series of rock pools. Nerves tangled in Tiggy's stomach just thinking about the ceremony and all those people who would watch her, but she tried to put on a brave face. It was Marina and Felipe's big moment too, and she didn't want to sour it with complaints.

Marina must have noticed Tiggy's anxious expression, because she hugged her arm and whispered, 'I'm a bit scared too.'

Tiggy sighed – a breathy laugh of relief. 'Thanks, Mari.'

After Diego had spent all of his coins on whipped sugar, his arms laden with a cloud of every colour, they made their way towards the makeshift wooden stage which rested near the back of the beach, nestled between the phoenix palms. Bunting and fresh flowers wreathed the platform, whilst lanterns swung from low-hanging boughs, blinking in time with the canopy of stars. Tiggy flushed at the thought of walking on stage to accept her medal of honour, but she swallowed down the tremor at the back of her throat. She had, after all, defeated the Pirate King. She could handle this.

A crowd began to gather as the brass band snaked its way from the bandstand to the wooden plinth at the front of the stage, their red uniforms glinting in the polished metal of their instruments.

Madre and Gabriella pushed towards the friends, the relief obvious in their broad smiles.

'Tiggy, dear-heart, you're on time,' Madre said.

Tiggy laughed. 'I promised I wouldn't be late, didn't I?'

'Triple promised,' Madre said. She glanced down at Diego and gasped, noticing the clumps of different-coloured sticky beet which erupted from his mouth and down his chin. 'Oh, Diego, the state of you.' She handed him an embroidered hand-kerchief, then turned to her daughter and smiled. 'Antigua, I have never been more proud. Just look at you.'

Tiggy wore breeches and a shirt, and had tied her cropped hair back with a blue bandanna. 'You think it suits me?'

'You look happy,' Madre replied, pulling her into a rose-scented hug, 'and that's all I ever wanted. I just wish your padre could see you. Our little girl, Guardian of the Ocean.' Tears sparkled on her cheeks.

'Hush,' Gabriella told Madre. 'Antigua is who she is because of her padre. Because of you. Her magic is tied to love, not hate, and that is why she chose to become Guardian rather than King.'

The ache of loss still made Tiggy's chest throb, yet she felt strangely content as she helped Madre dab her eyes.

'Quickly,' Gabriella said. 'The crew are waiting for you behind the stage. The Governor will call you up for your medals just as soon as he's said a few words.'

'And don't forget to say thank you,' Madre gushed. 'And curtsey . . . twice.'

Tiggy left Diego with Madre, and followed Marina and Felipe to the back of the stage, nodding politely to the townsfolk as they offered their thanks and praise.

The crew were huddled behind the stage, anxious expressions on their faces. They'd tried to spruce up for the occasion – Lucia and Cannon had brushed their hair, and Miguel, Doc and Spider wore bow ties, though they looked a little out of place balanced on top of their stained shirts. They beamed when they saw Tiggy, Marina and Felipe, and without speaking, the group formed a circle and placed their hands in the middle. 'Yo ho ho,' they whispered.

The brass band hiccupped to an abrupt stop and the crowd cheered as the Governor took centre stage – Tiggy could just make out the back of his ankles from where she stood.

As his father began to address the townsfolk, Salvador appeared, slipping between the palms, moving towards them like a serpent.

Marina grabbed Tiggy's arm. 'Tiggy, look. It's Salvador.' Her voice was an excited squeak.

Felipe groaned. 'What does *he* want?' He then grunted as Marina kicked him lightly on the shin.

Salvador approached Tiggy first, his moustache twitching as his mouth slid into a half-smile. He bowed neatly, as though hinged at the waist. 'Antigua, I thought I'd find you here.'

'Salvador,' she replied.

'I wanted to clear the air before the ceremony, and I thought how marvellous it would look if we led the first dance together.' He stifled a sly chuckle. 'We can avoid the brass band, just in case, you know, you lose your footing again.' He sniggered as he looked at her breeches.

Tiggy bristled. 'Thanks, Salvador, but I promised Felipe and Diego I'd dance with them.'

The crew giggled and Salvador scowled, even as he said, 'Of course, of course.' Undeterred, determined to save face, he turned toward the blushing Marina and nodded. Her eyes sparkled and she brushed down her frock.

'Ah, Marina,' he said. 'Such a pretty name, just like you.'

Miguel let out a loud guffaw and Lucia grimaced.

Salvador ignored them. '*You* wouldn't miss the opportunity to dance with the Governor's son, would you?' He glanced at the necklace around her neck and scowled. Only for a moment, but it was enough to show his true feelings about Marina's selkie heritage.

Marina touched the necklace defensively, though she never allowed her smile to slip. 'Why, thank you, Salvador.' She curtseyed. 'But I'm afraid I must politely decline. It's for your own good really, for I'm likely to turn into a seal, and that really would rather ruin it, all those flippers and whiskers . . . not really befitting of a gentleman.'

Salvador blinked, and his normally assured voice stumbled over his words. 'Er . . . right, right, of course not.' He bowed again, not entirely sure what to do. 'I'll, er, see you ladies later then.'

He backed away, still bowing, whilst Tiggy and her friends burst out laughing. They laughed so hard they missed their cue to walk on stage and receive their medals, and Tiggy ended up being late after all.

The next morning, Tiggy and the crew stood on the harbour, admiring the galleon. It had been repaired and painted by the people of Haven, and boasted the name: the *Resolute II*.

'I like it,' Lucia said.

'It has bigger guns,' Cannon replied, nodding.

'And more crow's-nests,' Spider said.

'And a surgeon's bench with extra medical tools,' Doc added.

Miguel sucked the air over his teeth. 'If you think we're letting you anywhere near us with them knives you are sorely mistaken.'

'It's perfect,' Tiggy said, a dreamy quality to her voice. 'Just what we need to roam the high seas.'

'And find all the treasure,' Spider added.

Tiggy scowled. 'And protect the sea creatures within and all who pass across its waves.'

'Oh yeah,' Spider replied with a wink. 'What she said.'

Lucia slung her arm around Spider's neck. 'We were rubbish traders, terrible fishermen, but we were even worse pirates. Helping the Guardian is what we were meant to do, isn't that right, Antigua?'

'Yes.' Tiggy reached out her hands and watched the turquoise light weave between her fingers. Maybe she could do this. After all, she had the ship's captain and crew by her side and the help of her favourite mermaid. She glanced at the scar which encircled the base of her hand like a strange, silvery bracelet – the place where Clara had pressed her own injured palm. Their link was now stronger than ever and, if they worked as a team, Tiggy knew that anything was possible.

She gazed across the port and smiled. It was slowly being rebuilt, with new ships arriving every day and the usual colours and sounds beginning to spill from its every corner. Across the harbour, towards the palms, she saw children playing on the beach as townsfolk dismantled the stalls from the carnival. Eventually, they would have enough confidence to dip their toes in the ocean, someday even swim within its waves. She had a lot of work to do, a lot of wrongs to make right, but she would use her magic for good and do her utmost to mend the rift between landlubbers and salt-drinkers.

She heard the excited cry of her little brother and turned to see her family and friends running along the harbour. They bounded up to her and scooped her into a mammoth hug.

Diego wriggled between them and held up Bobo. 'For you, in case you miss me.'

Tiggy took the faded bear and pressed it to her cheek for a moment. 'Thanks. But you keep him, as I need to know you're sleeping OK.'

Diego looked relieved and stuffed the teddy back into his pocket.

Madre squeezed her arms. 'I'm so sorry I asked you to change. Back at the ball, I mean. I was just so scared I'd lose you to the sea if I let you follow your heart.'

'You'll never lose me,' Tiggy replied, tears stinging her eyes.

Madre nodded and wiped her watery cheeks. 'Thank you, dear-heart.'

'What are we waiting for?' Felipe said, as he walked along the gangplank on to the ship. 'Has Cannon bagsied the best hammock?' He threw his canvas sack on to the deck.

'Bet your cannonballs she has,' Cannon replied, following him on board.

Tiggy turned to Marina. 'And you're sure you won't come?'

'I want to stay with Madre for now,' she replied. 'So I can learn more about the selkie ways.'

Gabriella smiled knowingly. 'She'll be able to visit you though, Tiggy. Anytime she wants.' The necklace around Marina's neck shimmered blue in the morning sun.

After one last round of kisses, Tiggy boarded the *Resolute II* and leant over the railings, waving to her loved ones and pretending not to cry.

Lucia gestured towards the railings at the bow of the ship. 'Care to do the honours, Guardian?'

Tiggy laughed. 'Aye aye, Captain.' She grabbed the rigging and hauled herself on to the bowsprit so she could look over the vast body of the galleon, the taste of salt on her lips and the sound of the waves in her heart. 'Man the helm, drop the sails. Come on, you dozy blighters. There be adventures to be had on them there high seas.'

And with the promise of adventure in its sails, the lure of mystery creaking through its hull, the great galleon began to move towards the ocean.

'Yo ho ho,' the crew roared, fists punching the air.

Yo ho ho, the ocean replied.

Acknowledgements

Just like a pirate ship, a book takes not one or two people to sail a true course and reach its destination, but an entire crew. This book is no exception. So let me start by thanking my co-captain, Oli Hyatt. Thank you so much for entrusting me with Tiggy and for writing this book with me, it's been a joy. Your energy and creativity is endless and I've loved the entire process.

I'd also like to thank all the lovely people at Chicken House. You're such a fab publisher, who genuinely cares about stories, authors and readers. Thank you for trusting me with yet another tale, and for introducing Oli and me. Special thanks to my editor, Kesia Lupo, who never fails to provide support, wisdom and ideas. I do so love working with you, you've nurtured me as a writer more than you realize. Huge thanks to Barry, whose understanding of children's literature is truly remarkable – thank you for your continued faith in me as a writer. Thanks to Esther Waller and Sue Cook for their fantastic proofreading skills, and a final thanks to Paola Escobar for this stunning cover

My darling family, thank you so much for all the

love, joy and laughter you have brought to my life. Simon Rainbow, you are my rock, Sweetheart. Thank you for reading all the drafts and listening to my constant book-babble, and thank you for being such a wonderful daddy to Fern and such a lovely step-dad to Ellie and Charlie. Without you, we would truly be lost at sea (and you thought I'd dropped the whole pirate ship analogy!). Ellie, Charlie and Fern, being your mum and watching you grow is the best thing in the world, you have taught me how to love without limits.

Thank you to my wonderful parents, not seeing you so much this year has been awful, but has also made me realize how lucky we are to have you so close. Thank you for always listening to my random book chat, and Dad, you will always be my secret plot-hole detector. And a final thanks to my lovely cousin, Lucy Fisher, who has held my hand (at a social distance) throughout covid.

I'd also like to thank my readers, who have given fantastic feedback on earlier drafts and helped shape this novel into the one you've just read. Special thanks to the younger readers, Lily Gilbert, Hannah Green and Alice Yates, your enthusiasm for Tiggy was such a boost – a gust of wind in the mainsail.

And to my adult readers and dear friends, Jenny Ellingford, Lucy Fisher, Helen Spencer, Heather Thompson, Gillian Waterworth (Mum) and Helen Yates (sis). I'm so grateful for your generous time, feedback and support.

A big thank you to my writing friends, Natali Drake (NJ Simmonds) and Shanna Alderliesten. Navigating the writing world is definitely more fun with you guys always on the other end of a phone. And to my lovely agent, Laura Williams, it's been so great working with you, and I can't wait to write more books with you as my champion and guide.

And finally, to you, lovely reader. May you always twine your magic with love and stories, and may you never drink congealed goat's milk. Yo ho ho!

Anna Rainbow

I first started writing about Tiggy twenty years ago, yet while the world and story expanded and developed, I struggled to write it because of my dyslexia. Every year I rewrote the first chapter, unable to convey the world and characters which were in my head.

However, a chance encounter with the effervescent Barry Cunningham and his team at Chicken House, and an introduction to the writing talent that is Anna Rainbow, gave Tiggy the opportunity to leave my head and hit the page. I will for ever be in their debt for believing in me. If writing a book is hard, writing a book with someone with learning difficulties, who was written off at school, must have felt like pulling teeth!

Barry you gave me my dream, Anna you made that dream come true.

I would like to thank my agent, Josephine Hayes. You are calm and ordered, while I'm an excitable mess of ideas and inconsistency. I tell everyone I'm next to Sir Chris Hoy on your website. One day I hope to beat him in a bike race.

Tiggy is based on my little sister, Beccy, so my biggest debt of gratitude goes to her. Beccy, I know sometimes it was hard growing up without always knowing where you fitted in. Even today, your hair is a bird's nest of knots and curls as you wander through life with your great big heart and no shoes on your feet. Now you have a beautiful family, three smashing little boys, and a big brother who is immensely proud of you.

I would like to thank Emma, for supporting me on my many adventures. I know it's not always easy! You are a round hole and I am a square peg but we somehow fit together beautifully! I admire you more than you know as a woman, a mother, a professional and a wife. I love the awkward way you love me and the free way you love our boys. Lockdown has been a blessing that has meant I get to see more of you and I've loved it.

Bugsy you're the most caring little thing, you bring joy to all that meet you and tackle life in the most open enthusiastic way possible. You inspire me to do the same.

Ziggy you are a cheeky monkey, but you have a hug that lights up my heart and you make me laugh every day! You're an intense, direct boy that never does anything in half measures – I'm afraid you got Daddy's genes! So good luck!

Mum, Dad, Peg, Chazzer, Matt, Emma, Rhain,

Otis, Yuuki, Xander and Lollypop . . . Now I've written a book based on one of our family, watch out, none of you are safe!!

And to the readers, I really hope you enjoy reading about Tiggy's epic voyage of self-discovery. Writing it has been a labour of love. Perhaps it will encourage you to share your ideas and adventures, and I very much hope to read them one day.

Oli Hyatt